DOUBLES

To
Jon
7.13.10

DOUBLES

a novel

NIC BROWN

COUNTERPOINT
BERKELEY

An excerpt appeared in *Washington Square*.

Library of Congress Cataloging-in-Publication Data
Brown, Nic, 1977–
  Doubles : a novel / by Nic Brown.
    p. cm.
  ISBN 978-1-58243-507-7
  1. Tennis players—Fiction. I. Title.
  PS3602.R72242D68 2010
  813'.6—dc22

                              2010003259

Cover design by Silverander Communications
Interior design by Pauline Neuwirth, Neuwirth & Associates, Inc.

Printed in the United States of America

COUNTERPOINT
2117 Fourth Street
Suite D
Berkeley, CA 94710

www.counterpointpress.com

Distributed by Publishers Group West

10 9 8 7 6 5 4 3 2 1

For
Abby and Frances

DOUBLES

part

1

1

AT THE SERVICE line I started to count.

One

Because when I was young,

Two

I got too nervous at the line.

Three

I'd freeze.

Four

I'd just stand there in terror, waiting for the right moment.

Five

So I was taught to count

Six

to nine before each toss.

Seven

Ever since, I couldn't serve without counting.

Eight

Even when the other side of the net was empty and I was alone on a public court, serving for the first time in five months.

Nine

Before the accident, I had been, I knew without bragging, among the best tennis players in the world. I reached a world ranking of 17. Third in the U.S. Only the Simon brothers were ahead of me. And they didn't count. In Chennai in 2005, my serve was clocked at 148 miles per hour, the third fastest ever recorded at an ATP event. You probably think I appeared on television, in newspapers, won large cash prizes. And you would be wrong. Because that's what singles players do.

I play doubles.

When I was younger I played singles, but doubles had found me like a job recruiter lurking in the shadows of my dreams. I didn't know one doubles player who had actually set out to be one. We were all a bit older, or smaller, or perhaps with weaker groundstrokes. Less stamina. Maybe we peaked late. A lot of us had gone to college—the death knell for a tennis career. Regardless, we'd all tried our hand at singles and failed in some form or another. But we had our own unique skills. I had beaten lots of top singles players when they moonlighted in doubles, names people knew, usually trying to get some extra time on the court to help their singles game, or help out a young player from their country, or just earn some extra cash. I beat Andre Agassi twice. I beat Roger Federer in 2002 at San Jose. Chang. Rafter. These wins never made headlines. You could tell, when these guys lost they didn't care. Doubles wins, doubles losses. To them it was still only doubles.

It was the counting at the service line that earned me my name. An adjective for a name. An adjective to describe the way people thought of me, I guess. Because it had stuck since age six, when my doubles partner, Kaz—who was my partner for more than two decades—had gotten so frustrated at the net waiting for me to serve that he just started to yell one of the few English words he knew: "Slow! Slow! Slow!" In the years since, Kaz's vocabulary improved, but Slow—the adjective for sloths, snails, and turtles—stuck.

The pink ball was now a dark orb rising against the May sky. One bit of lint parted from the felt and drifted away on the breeze. The ball reached its apogee, and I swung. The racquet carried me forward, lunging into the court. The ball hit the top of the frame with a wet thud, missing the strings altogether. I staggered to a stop near midcourt as the ball traveled in a lazy high arc over the chain-link fence to my right, bounced three times, and settled into the grass.

All earthbound routes to the ball were blocked by chain-link or webs of growth. Trees and vines and hidden wonders of nature swelled into any open space.

So I started to climb.

Five feet, ten, the ridiculous fence stood at least twenty feet tall. I had almost reached its top when I was stopped by the sight of a turtle. He was a large, loping thing that in warm weather appeared in assorted spots throughout the neighborhood, in one place before lunch and then blocks away by the time you left the house, leaving you to wonder whether he traveled at a secret fast gear when no one was looking. My wife and I had moved him out of the street dozens of times. On my birthday two years ago she had written our names onto its back in red fingernail polish. I had held him in the air, all appendages hidden within that mobile chamber until the legs emerged, clawing in circles as Anne brushed her red polish onto his back. ANNE HEARTS SLOW. The message was chipped but still legible now, even from my perch.

I clung to the fence and watched. The turtle stretched his beak close to the orb, as if he were smelling it, then turned towards me. But it wasn't me that he was interested in. It was the sound of car wheels crunching over gravel in the lane behind me.

I turned as a pair of bull horns emerged from the vegetation. Then a chrome grille, one muddy tire, a dented green door, a black dog in the passenger seat, and finally my old coach, Manny LaSalle, towering behind the wheel of a dusty green 1980 Fiat Spider convertible.

"Slow," he said. "Get down."

"I'm getting my ball."

"You only have one ball?"

Manny stepped out of the miniature car, his legs extending slowly, one joint at a time. He was close to six and a half feet tall and all bones and angles. Because of body type alone, we were often mistaken for brothers. Other than unusual height, though, we looked nothing alike. I'm a wisp of man, thinner even than Manny. People who learned I was a professional athlete often thought I was joking. My receding hairline, inset front teeth, and sunken cheeks gave me the look of having just come out of a prolonged sickness. But I hadn't been sick. It's just what I looked like. Manny's hair, on the other hand, was kept in a black pompadour, and as he entered the court it stood up in a type of hair explosion. He was dressed like an emaciated cowboy in a black Western shirt, tight Wranglers, and cowboy boots, which made his spider legs seem that much longer. The strangest thing about Manny, though, were his lips. They were huge. On his long, thin face, they seemed out of context, comic and swollen. He had once told me that his own mother said his mouth looked like an inflamed butthole. He had never been a real coach, just a failed college player who had dropped out and traveled around with me as a hitting partner, offering advice and driving his old VW Vanagon from U.S. challenger to U.S. challenger, stringing racquets in parking lots for extra cash. He hadn't worked since the accident. Nobody wanted him but me.

As he stepped onto the court, the dog did not follow. It sat in the passenger seat, looking up towards the leaves, licking air. Manny ignored him. The dog was just part of his aura.

"Slow," he said. "Safety first."

I maintained my hold on the fence and said, "What are you doing here?"

Manny lived in New York. I lived in North Carolina. I had not been expecting him. He picked up the racquet and began hitting it against his palm. It was a child's racquet, half size and fuchsia. I had found it leaning against the fence while on a walk. The tennis ball beside it was pink and had been half submerged in a puddle.

"This is cute," he said.

"I'm sick of people coming to check on me."

"I'm not here to chéck on you. I'm in town because I have to file all this bullshit."

"What happened?"

"Slow, is that ball pink?"

Manny never answered questions. You could ask him anything, and he would still give you whatever answer he wanted. Or no answer at all.

"What happened?"

"It is, isn't it?"

"What *happened*?"

"Slow, you know I love her."

"Who?"

"Katie."

I did know. Years of my childhood had been spent watching her walk down the street in the late afternoon, wearing damp Umbros, coming from the pool, a towel over her shoulder while golf clubs clacked in the distance and open windows released the stuttered scales of piano lessons. We'd been in the same class, and she occupied my middle school fantasies. High school. After. It was impossible not to love her. At times I thought there'd never been a love so pure. She was now a lawyer who represented a number of art galleries in New York, defending the rights of paintings that I could have done blindfolded, sculptures of gorillas made from toilet paper. It was as foreign a world to me as I imagined tennis was to her. In 1999 she had married Manny in a union I thought I might never comprehend, a validation that he had everything I lacked. A failed player, but successful in all other realms—and he got the girl.

"Yeah, but *what happened*?" I said. I tightened my grip. My fingers were beginning to ache, but I wasn't going to move. Lately, I had been sleeping past 2:00 PM. I cried when Al Gore accepted his Academy Award. I didn't return phone calls. I had let myself slide into indulgence. But I didn't want to come down. I felt that, if I could just hold on to that fence, I was still in control of this conversation; that, even though my coach—the one person who had told me to do more things than anyone else in my life—was standing below, directing me down, that I was the director of this scene. My fingers remained braided between wire.

"I'm not going to tell you the whole thing," Manny said. "But I do need to tell you this one part. So I get drunk at Rudy's the other night, and then on my way home this group of girls on the sidewalk is all like, 'Take our picture?' And one of them is this girl I've been wanting to get in there with for a long time, so I take her home. She looks like Scarlett Johansson. In the face," he said, then traced an hourglass into the air with the racquet. "She's healthy."

"What about Katie?"

"Well, my phone starts ringing the next morning, and I just don't answer it."

"Wait. Where was she?"

"We'd already broken up, a few days before. This was after. But so the phone keeps ringing, and then the next thing I hear is the key in the door. Yeah. It's Katie. She's like, 'You're here with somebody, aren't you.' And I'm naked. You know she was all like, 'What's up, donkey dick?' I don't say anything, and she leaves. I pick up my phone after the door closes and see that she'd been texting me. The first one said, 'I've been calling. I think you're with somebody.' And the last one said, 'I'm coming over. If you're with somebody, I'm going to do you both.' So I just sort of, without thinking, just text her back and say, 'Come back.' And she says, 'Why?' And I say, 'Why not?' So then she comes back. Steps in and the first thing she does is walk up to the bed, where Scarlett is, and kisses her. Katie calms her down, says all this stuff, and starts taking off her clothes. And Slow, it was just. So natural. It was like, that was the way it was meant to be. And it wasn't nasty or anything. I mean, it was nasty. But it was just. It was nice."

Katie Barshaw? Who had once told me the craziest thing she could think of was taking a shower outside, in the sprinkler, in a bathing suit? I was only thirty, and my friends had become unrecognizable.

Manny twirled the racquet on his index finger. It spun perfectly, a blur of fuchsia and white. I moved my hands to new diamonds of wire, alleviating the deepening ache in my fingers for a few seconds as I tried to process what he was telling me.

"Slow, I gotta tell you, man. It was a great experience. And after that, I mean, we just felt so connected. I mean, everything was on the table. *Everything* was on the table. It was like, we had just gone through it all together, you know? There were no secrets."

"So you're back together?"

Manny stopped the racquet in midspin. "She got into my emails."

"Who were you emailing?"

He squinted up at me, the sun full on his face.

"Come down!"

"Who'd you email?"

"You ever read those personals on Craigslist?"

In fact, I had been looking for a moped that very morning and had clicked on the personals on Craigslist, just out of curiosity. It was a litany of bizarre sexual requests, people inviting strangers to come over for anonymous spankings, threesomes, husbands wanting to watch strangers have sex with their bound wives. I couldn't stop reading.

"No," I said, meaning yes. He knew what I meant. Sometimes I felt like I didn't even have to speak with him, that we could converse in silence. We had spent so much time together in cars, planes, hotel rooms, locker rooms. I had heard others formed bonds like this. Golfers and their caddies. Soldiers. Bands on tour. Theater troupes.

It was the summer camp syndrome, the creation of your own move-able world; insular, intimate, and intense. Unknowable to anyone but those within its invisible boundaries. But this I had to ask: "Anybody ever come over?"

"No," he said. "Well yeah, this one girl came over once." He waved his hand in the air as if it were nothing. "But nobody responds to those things. I mean, nobody thinks those personals are real." Then he looked up at me, squinting into the sun, and said, "But they're real."

The neighborhood was absolutely silent, save for one basketball bouncing off the concrete court of a hidden, distant driveway.

"But so I had to come down and file this bullshit for the divorce, and now I'm heading back up. Forest Hills is this week. Kaz can't play without you."

Divorce seemed inevitable with anyone married to Manny, but still I was shocked at the word. I tried to keep it in check. I said, "He knows I can't play."

"He needs you there for all his voodoo shit."

"I have to work."

"My God," Manny said. He turned to the dog, as if he might under-stand. "You believe this?"

Manny would never let something like work get in the way. Everyone I knew was tumbling headfirst with momentum. Winning tournaments, taking road trips, having sex with multiple women.

"Come on," Manny said.

I considered another week by myself, answering emails, going to sleep at 9:00. I looked around, and the turtle had disappeared, replaced by a small girl in jeans with an elastic waistband who had suddenly appeared in the gravel road. She said, "You got my racquet."

"Here," Manny said and held it towards her.

She looked him in the face and stepped back.

"What?" he said. "Here."

She started to run.

"Wait! It's right here!" Manny said. He held the racquet out towards the empty road, then raised both hands into the air. "What the fuck?" He looked up at me like I should understand. "That girl is totally getting her parents. Come *on*."

He started to climb. The fence shook as he neared. I was amazed that he could climb in those boots. The toes were just narrow enough to wedge into the fence, and with his freakish limbs he closed in quickly.

"Leave me alone," I said.

He stopped only once he was beside me.

"Hi," he said.

Right then a buzzard, a huge, black, oily thing, landed opposite us on the fence. It outstretched a set of wings that spread more than six feet, warming them in the sunlight.

Manny shook his head and whispered, "This is not a good sign."

The turtle emerged from the brush at the side of the road, pressing through gravel as it inched across the little street, but the buzzard just stayed on the fence with its wings outstretched. It didn't want that turtle until it was dead.

As long as I held on, I was master of this situation. I didn't want to compromise. I didn't want to rush. It was the sort of sane, clinical thinking that had earned me an adjective for a name.

One

The buzzard's outstretched wings caught the breeze, slowly pushing the bird back and forth.

Two

I looked at Manny. His oversize lips were chapped. His forehead was sunburnt.

Three

I wanted to see Kaz.

Four

I wanted to see Katie.

Five

Six

Seven

"Hello?" Manny said and reached for me.

Eight

He pulled at my shoulders, trying to pry me off.

Nine

I'd seen Manny's face in so many continents over so many years. How many times had he told me to hit ten more serves? Ten in a row and then we can go. How many times had he told me to wake up, put ice on this, stretch it, move your feet. It's your feet! Those giant lips were made to command. But I wanted this decision to be mine.

Then, out of nowhere, a woman said, "Excuse me?"

I looked down. It was the lady who walked her Dalmatian around the neighborhood every day while wearing a Lowe's apron filled with plastic bags.

"I told you," Manny said.

"You take my daughter's racquet?" the woman said.

"Nope," Manny said.

She stepped into the court and picked up the tennis racquet, then held it before her: evidence. "There's a leash law, you know."

"He's a good boy."

"I'm calling the police."

"It's a public court!" Manny said.

"I know you," she said. "You're the tennis player."

"OK," I said.

"I don't care who you are. This is a family neighborhood."

She walked rapidly away, disappearing beyond the vegetation.

"Slow," Manny said. He put his hand back on my shoulder and started to pull.

"Just let me think."

One

"You're scaring the neighbors."

Two

Three

"You don't look good, Slow."

Four

"You can't stay on this fence. It hurts."

Five

"Ow! Goddamn."

Six

Seven

Eight

Nine

Then I counted again. Manny couldn't get me off. I was on my ninth three when I first heard the sirens. I let my aching fingers slip out of those diamonds of galvanized wire and fell, my old coach tumbling through the air behind me. As we descended, the buzzard leapt, flapping his giant wings with a sloppy, hollow clutter, and for a brief moment we were all airborne above that tennis court, floating through the only sunlight in the neighborhood.

We landed and ran. Across the gravel we ducked into the thick brush.

One police car slowly rolled across the gravel and stopped beside Manny's Fiat. I couldn't believe he had been in town with me for less than ten minutes and already we were hiding from the police.

"It's legally parked," he whispered. "Isn't it?"

A large young black woman stepped out of the cruiser and wiped her glistening forehead. She looked into the Fiat, her large rear end straining the polyester of her pants as she bent. The dog calmly turned to look at her. She circled the car, inspecting it closely from different angles, then took out a notepad and started to write.

"Wait!" Manny yelled and stood. "Hey!" He emerged from the woods with his hands up.

"Who are you?"

"That's public parking."

"I say it wasn't?"

Manny stood in silence, his arms still in the air.

"What you doing in the bushes?"

"I thought you were after us."

"Mrs. Sampson been wasting my time for years. This your Fiat?"

"Yes, ma'am."

"You thinking about selling it?"

"That's my baby."

"My husband's been looking for one of these forever. Can I give you my number?"

As the woman wrote her information onto her pad, Manny said, "Come out, Slow."

I didn't move.

"Slow, it's fine," he said, then turned back to the policewoman and shook his thumb over his shoulder. "My friend's still in the bushes," he said in a dramatic stage whisper. "Bad few months."

It had been a bad few months. But I hadn't felt so alive during any of them. And I wanted to feel alive. So I stood up. I brushed the leaves off my sweatpants and patted down a few wisps of hair. My coach was right here; my partner was in New York, waiting. We had a dog and a Fiat, and the sun was shining. I stepped over one Doritos bag, two empty orange Gatorade bottles, and a plastic grocery bag half melted into the ground—surely filled with the droppings of some neighborhood dog—and pushed aside one low-hanging live oak branch. I felt good. I felt invincible. I stepped into the light, and Manny and the police officer turned. I was going to Forest Hills.

2

I STOOD BY my kitchen sink, the only spot inside that got cell phone reception, and watched Manny and the dog sun themselves on the porch. Manny had taken his shirt off, and each rib was outlined by shadowed flesh, sparse chest hairs plastered down with sweat. We had escaped the grip of the law. I felt drunk with the rush of adrenaline.

My boss squeaked hello to me from the other end of the phone line. He was named Steve Como, and he had a combover, and everyone called him Steve Combover. Not to his face. He had been my manager when I was on tour. For the past month and a half I had been doing publicity for him, writing copy, press releases, and player guides, fielding calls from sportswriters who wanted to set up interviews or get tickets. It was basically forwarding emails and arranging times and taking down phone numbers. It was a charity gig that they gave me after the accident, and I did almost all of it from home. I didn't know when I'd be back on tour, Combover knew I wasn't playing, and I knew he wanted me to be occupied. It wasn't a bad idea. At some point I'd have to get a real job. Doubles could sustain me for only so long. Combover had a voice like a creaky door. He was divorced, and his three daughters all lived with him. At his Fourth of July party he'd smoked marijuana on his patio and then started to cry. I liked him very much.

I said, "George Vecsey just emailed me."

Vecsey was a columnist for *The Times*. He was revered. I had never spoken to him in my life. I probably never would. But he had just emailed, or at least his assistant had, asking if I could send him a photo of Tim Wheeler, a teenage client of ours.

"About what?" Combover said.

"He wants to talk about Tim getting a wildcard into the French. In person."

"No."

"Yeah." I let that sit for a second. That part was the lie. I could almost hear Combover's mind moving numbers. Tennis players never had real managers. Only the top guys, really. Combover was just an ambitious accountant. The company ran on low salaries out of a dingy office in a Pittsboro strip mall.

He said, "Tim's not getting it."

"He might."

"In New York?"

"Yeah."

"We can't afford it."

"I have a ride."

"With who?"

"Manny."

"Jesus Christ."

"It'll be fine."

"No."

"I just need a card for expenses."

"*No.*"

"Steve, I need this."

Steve Combover. I guess he was just too nice. Three hours later I was riding in the passenger seat of Manny's Fiat with a black dog in my lap and Combover's credit card in my pocket.

Manny kept the speed well above the limit as we drove from Pittsboro back into Chapel Hill. He always seemed employed by life, close to the source. His recklessness was innate. In high school, he specialized in car surfing, the practice of standing atop a moving car with arms outstretched, surfing the pavement swells of Chapel Hill. He fell off the roof of his Mitsubishi and knocked out his front teeth in the eleventh grade. He wrecked three cars before he was twenty.

"Did you file?" he said, south of the Chatham County line.

"Yeah. I filed."

You stop playing for any sort of injury, and you can file for a protective ranking. What this does, if the ATP approves it, is it freezes your points. Points are what you amass for every tournament win. Their total yields your ranking. And your ranking determines what tournaments you get into. So points are everything. But the thing about points is, they only last for fifty-two weeks. One year. Which means you have to win the same tournaments every year if you just want to keep your ranking the same, let alone raise it. An injury, without protected points, means the points just disappear, week after week, tournament after tournament. But even though I wasn't the one who had actually been injured, the former strength trainer for the UNC soccer team had written a letter to the ATP for me saying that I'd injured my back. They don't send private detectives to confirm these things. They just approve or they don't. In my case, they did. So I was frozen at 32 in the world. I had another five weeks before I could even start to use it.

"Where you playing first?" Manny said.

"I don't know."

"Why?"

"Because I'm enjoying living like a human. Eating and drinking normal. Sleeping."

"I always watered you, Slow."

"I'm serious."

"What? How do humans eat?"

"Remember when I ate the mayonnaise?" I said, because one morning I'd woken up in Manny's van and gotten out while he was still asleep. I wanted a place to eat, but I had no idea where we were. We were parked behind a long line of loading docks. I kept walking, but I couldn't even get out of the loading area. I finally just got back into the van, and under the seat I found a jar of warm mayonnaise that we'd taken from a player lounge at some point. And so I ate four large spoonfuls of mayonnaise.

Manny nodded, pursing his huge lips. "You hate mayonnaise."

"That's not what I'm saying."

Manny was driving so close to the bumper of a chrome tanker that I felt like I was going to vomit. So I said, "You're driving so close to the bumper of that tanker that I think I'm going to vomit."

"It's sucking me in, Slow," Manny said, gazing at the Fiat warped and inverted on the back of that glimmering tank. "Pull me out. Pull me out! Eject."

"I'm serious."

He squinted his dark eyes at me. "Talk to me, goose. You been in a car since?"

I shook my head. Because no, I had not. I had not been in a car since.

"Where is she?"

"Same place."

Manny slowed while entering the next intersection, then turned left on Manning Drive. He dropped the Fiat into second and whirred up the steep hill. My house was two miles in the opposite direction. But I knew where we were going. At the top of the hill, past the construction that seemed perpetual on this end of campus, stood the maze of buildings and covered walkways and parking lots and tunnels (that I had once heard stretched underground for four solid blocks) that was collectively University Hospital.

3

IN THE SPRING of my senior year, when I was ranked eighth in the country for collegiate singles, Manny threw a birthday party for himself on his pontoon. It was a wide, cream-colored platform atop two missile-shaped floats. A roof of corrugated metal painted in green and blue stripes covered half of it. We dropped anchor in Jordan Lake only a few dozen yards out of the shaded cove of the dock.

After an hour of Coors Light and Frito Lays, I maneuvered myself beside a tall, thin woman who wore a red vintage bathing suit with a small ruffle approximating a skirt around her narrow hips. A white swim cap blossomed in bright rubber flowers around her head. Goggles rested on her forehead. She appeared to have come from central casting for bather, circa 1930. Her skin was so fair it worried me to see it in direct sunlight. Together we turned our eyes to the sky.

Manny stood on the pontoon roof. He was naked, save for a wide straw hat. The thin metal sagged under his feet. He held both hands in the air, as if conjuring a spirit out of Jordan Lake. Voices rose from the platform below. Jump! Jump! He lifted the hat from his head and threw it spinning into the summer sky. A lit cigarette dangled from his giant lips as he leapt into the air. His long, thin frame arced gracelessly towards the water, legs and torso at a sloppy angle like he was going to fold in on himself. Against the bright blue of the sky, his penis dangled beneath him in a thin silhouette.

Water splashed us as he landed. The woman and I leaned over. All that was left on the surface was a cigarette atop the roiling entrance, joined one moment later by the slowly spinning hat.

A breeze blew across the lake, and the woman held herself against the chill. She said, "Adam!"

A young man with a shaved head held up a hand as if to simply acknowledge that the woman had spoken, then turned back to the water.

"You cold?" I said. It was what I had been building up to.

She didn't answer. She just held herself tighter. Then, after a few moments, as if she had just noticed I was there, she said, "Oof. It's cold."

"You want my shirt?" I said and held up the sleeve of the flannel shirt tied around my waist. Again, she didn't answer, just turned back to the water. Manny emerged and spit a high stream of water from his mouth.

"Adam!" she said, but this time he didn't respond. Then she turned to me and said, "You drive?"

"Me?"

"Yeah. You give me a ride?"

I looked around. "Now?"

"Yeah. These people suck."

I knew almost all of them. Most were on the team. But Manny always said, "If you're excited, you're invited." So there were strangers. Like Adam. And like her.

"I guess," I said. "I'm Slow, by the way." She didn't seem to hear me. She said, "Can I see your teeth?"

"Excuse me?"

"Smile."

I smiled.

"Yeah, see how they're set back? You have very nice teeth. I love teeth like that."

I ran my tongue across my teeth. I felt incapable of saying the correct thing. I looked around again. All eyes were on the other side of the boat, watching Manny.

"So we're cool? You going to Chapel Hill?"

"Yeah."

"Alright." She turned and outstretched her arms, hands together, as if teaching a child how to dive. If a line had extended from her fingertips, it would have stretched to the horizon, cutting through the hot air wavering just above the expanse of cool water, passing over Greensboro, crossing the Appalachian Mountains, and shooting across the miles of airspace filled with insects, low-flying birds, and tennis balls tossed for serves. She then raised her arms above her head and held herself in a straight, upright line before she tipped forward and dove.

Kaz stepped away from an oxidized aluminum cooler and said, "Get her name?"

I shook my head, watching the water. It still held her.

If Manny or Kaz had their eyes on a girl, one of them was going to get her. I did not engage in competition. There was never a selection in my favor. But I was happy to assist. They were the ones who had told me to get her name. I had a doubles partner, a scholarship, and my serve. Tennis was my focus, my friends were part of the focus, and everything else was peripheral. At twenty-one, I was already going bald and was still a virgin. Tennis—the partner, the coach, and the game—these were the basics and the nourishment. They could have the girls. Danger in my life was provided by late comebacks, dangerous second serves, and the debauchery of Manny and Kaz. I had ceded them my own.

But when the rubber flowers blossomed through the surface, followed by that long, blinking white face, and she said, "Coming?" I dove.

Manny was midway up the small ladder that hung from the boat into the water. He dangled by one hand, a foot propped on a step, and looked at us over his shoulder.

"Mutiny!" he shouted. "Theft!"

Kaz put his hands in the air in disbelief.

I rolled back underwater and, in that cool space below the wavering heat, smiled.

In the parking lot the girl stopped, barefoot and dripping on the gravel. She pointed and said, "That's my favorite car."

"The Dart?"

She nodded. "You ever seen one?"

"A Dart?"

"They're my favorite."

"That's mine."

"No."

"Yes."

"No."

"Yes!" I laughed.

I admired her long, reedlike body as she ran her finger in one slow motion along the crest of the hood and circled the machine. She was even more beautiful than the car. It was the only car I'd ever owned. It was not often admired. My mother bought it for me out of the back of the newspaper when I was fifteen years old. At the time, to me, it had looked exotic. Fast. It was, of course, neither. For fifteen years it was the most consistent space in my life. My family had sold the house I grew up in. The town had expanded to the point that areas were unrecognizable. My high school had been demolished. Streets that I used to ride my bike on were now four lanes wide with speed limits above 45. The Dart, though, it had always been there. It still even smelled the same.

We headed back towards Chapel Hill on Wade Avenue, nearing the State Fairgrounds and I-40, past nondescript one-story brick buildings with no doors, no windows, their walls grown over with kudzu. I drove slowly and without speaking, glad for the wind roaring through the windows. It was very seldom that I rode with a girl in the Dart. The last had been Katie, who had asked me to teach her how to serve during her summer vacation. I had driven her to the tennis center in terrified silence, embarrassed by the sputtering, growling engine. Once on court, I was fine. I spoke, I helped her with her toss, with her follow-through, and, for a moment, I thought I might have a chance with this girl who had had me charmed since childhood. Back in the Dart, though, I became meek and mute and useless. I was determined that wouldn't happen again today.

The girl said, "Have you seen the Monet show?"

I followed her gaze down a side road and shook my head, trying to act like I knew what she was talking about. "It's good," she said. "Except for the timed tickets." I let the wind overtake us again and turned back to the road. In the center of the lane before us stood a small man with stringy black hair, a plaid shirt, and tight black jeans. He was waving his arms over his head. I braked hard, and the car began to skid. The trunk slid towards the shoulder. The man just stood there impatiently, as if he wanted me to come closer, faster. When the car finally ceased to move, we were only a few yards away from him. He jogged towards us and opened the passenger-side door.

"Thanks," he said, panting. His voice was oddly high-pitched. He sat on the backseat. "Car broke down."

"Oh. OK," I said, stunned that this person was now in my car. He smelled like wood smoke and mud.

"What are you doing?" the girl said.

"Lady, you almost drove over me."

A dusty green Mercedes appeared in the lane behind me and honked two sharp bursts. I touched the accelerator.

"Sorry," I said, as we picked up speed.

"Going to High Point," he said. In the rearview, I watched him run his hands through his hair, thin and tangled and greasy. Tattoos crawled across several narrow fingers.

"We're only going to Chapel Hill."

"I need to get to High Point."

The girl put her hands in the air, as if holding a large invisible ball, and shook her head. She snorted in disgust.

"Hey, huffy," he said. "Got a problem?"

I turned to the girl, and my gaze seemed to wake her. She said, "What?"

"I said, you got a problem with me?"

She turned around and looked at him. "I can't hear what you're saying."

"You deaf?"

"Yes."

They stared at each other.

"Really?"

"Yeah. I'm hard of hearing."

"This your girlfriend?" the guy said.

"No."

Two helicopters flew low overhead, their roar pulsing through the Dart.

He said, "I like her."

I had never picked up a hitchhiker in my life. We drove past a strip mall filled with antique cars, their owners sitting on folding chairs by popped hoods. Several heads turned as we passed, a few reaching into the air to wave. It made me feel safe. I waved back. Having this man in the car was something Manny would have done, and if Manny did something, girls usually liked it, and so I was going to do this, and this girl was going to like it.

"What do you do?" The man said. He spoke in exaggerated volume.

The girl didn't answer.

"What does she do?" the man said to me, still excessively loud.

"I don't know."

"You don't know?"

"We just met."

"Well then, see?" he said, almost screaming over the wind. "We aren't so different, my dear."

"I hear you, asshole," she said. "I work at an art museum."

"The one back there?" Even he knew more about art than I did.

The girl shook her head. "Chapel Hill."

"Cultured. I like it. What about you? Let me guess. College?"

My face warmed.

"And you two been swimming?" he said.

"Yeah," I said.

"I know. You know how? I read minds."

"Clearly took a mind reader," the girl said.

The man's face, thin and deeply wrinkled in vertical creases along his cheeks, jiggled in the rearview mirror along with each fluctuation in the pavement. He met my eyes in the reflection.

"You play tennis," he said.

"Wrong," the girl said.

"Not you."

For a second I thought perhaps the man recognized me. *The Daily Tar Heel* ran my photo two weeks earlier when I'd beaten Cov Deramus, the national number 2 from Virginia. I had been recognized then, but that was on campus.

"He just found some tennis balls rolling around back there," I said.

"Maybe I did, maybe I didn't. But you . . . I know about you too. You like to take pictures. Polaroid pictures."

The girl turned her bare shoulder and leaned over the seat. Her spine stood out in sharp relief, fine hair on each disk glowing in the sunlight through the passenger side. She stretched one long, thin arm to her small, yellow canvas tote bag and lifted it from the cushion beside the man. He laughed.

"Four for four. What do you shoot?"

"Don't you know?" she said, pushing a large Polaroid camera deeper into her bag. He laughed again. "I take pictures of the truth."

"Whoa. Arty," he said. "And I'll tell you something else. You're both from Chapel Hill, but you don't know each other? That's weird if you ask me."

"She didn't grow up in Chapel Hill," I said.

"Yeah I did."

"Where'd you go to school?"

"Friends School."

"It true you guys didn't wear shoes to class?"

She nodded.

"And didn't have grades?"

"Evaluations. Where'd you go?"

"Durham Academy."

"So," the man said. "You're rich, but so are you."

We passed a large blinking road sign that read NC STATE PRISON IN VICINITY. DO NOT PICK UP HITCHHIKERS.

He pointed and said, "I just got out of there."

I fingered the top of the gearshift and tried to keep my eyes on the road. The traffic was stopped in the lane ahead of us, and I slowly rolled to a stop. I couldn't tell if the guy was joking.

"What is it?" the girl said, leaning her head out the open window.

"I don't know," I said.

She stepped out of the car.

"Hey," I said, but she kept going. She had had no response to the man's announcement that he was a recently released convict. I couldn't tell if she hadn't heard or just didn't care.

On the shoulder she put one hand on her forehead to shield her eyes from the sun. She was still in her bathing suit, a large, red towel wrapped high around her hips. She looked stunning and out of place, like a marble sculpture placed on the moon.

"She is into you," the guy said. "I'm serious. Let me help you out. She was watching you the whole time you were at the lake."

"How'd you know we were at the lake?"

"I told you," he said, and pointed at his temple. "Seriously, play it cool with this girl. I'll help you out."

We sat in silence for several long seconds. A surprising calm came over the stopped cars. There were no horns, no shouting, just the quiet rumble of the Dart's low idle.

"You really just get out of jail?" I said.

"Yeah."

"What for?"

"Mortgage fraud."

The girl returned to the car and opened the door.

"I couldn't see anything," she said, sitting back down. "It's backed up for a ways." She turned on the radio. "I love music in the car." "Girls Just Want to Have Fun" by Cyndi Lauper squeezed out of my mono speaker. She turned up the volume until it hurt. "It's the only place I can ever really hear it!"

In the rearview the man raised his eyebrows and reached for the door. He stepped into the road and stretched his arms towards the sky. He was extremely short and thin, like a greasy matador in black jeans. As soon as the door closed behind him, the girl said, "We've got to get rid of him."

"Shhh," I said, but it was too late. She had basically yelled it. The man looked back at us with a wide smile.

I would drop him off at a gas station in Chapel Hill. We'd be fine. I wanted to be dangerous and calm. I didn't want her to know how scared I actually was.

Behind her, on the shoulder, I saw the man call out something to the car in front of us. It was a champagne Grand Marquis, the driver's head low and gray. The man grimaced and turned his ear as if listening to a response. Then he picked up a small rock and threw it into the side of the car. At an exaggerated slow pace he began his return to the Dart. The gray hair in front of us turned. I could just barely see the face of an old man. It was filled with terror and confusion. The girl hadn't seen any of it though, and when she finally turned to see what I was looking at, the man was already opening the door.

"It's moving up ahead," he said.

Traffic began to creep. Fifty yards ahead, a young man stood beside a yellow Jeep Wrangler on the side of the road speaking into his cell phone. As we passed, I saw a red smear across the pavement leading to a deer crumpled on the side of the road, antlers twisting its neck at a sharp angle, horn tangled into the wavering heat. We passed three dilapidated tobacco hangers overgrown with kudzu. A pickup truck filled with young Mexican children drove by us, the boys all facing towards the center of the truck bed, where the head of a German shepherd emerged. The boys all reached for it, petting it, rubbing it, like the dog were some highway celebrity. They pushed and laughed, one reaching over the other trying to get to the animal.

"Your dad runs that art museum," the man said.

The girl cocked her head, like she had heard some distant sound.

"How'd you know that?"

"Five for five."

"And you . . ." He pointed at me, his long, boney finger wavering in the air behind my seat. He then circled the finger, as if winding a long string around it, and flung his hand upward. "Your daddy is a lawyer."

As he said it, the dog leapt from that pickup truck. I watched in the rearview as it landed hard on the pavement, rolled onto the shoulder, and, in one smooth motion, popped up and started to run. Within seconds it disappeared into the kudzu. The children banged on the truck's back windshield, trying to make the driver stop. I thought to myself, *If I fell from a truck bed, I would surely crumple into a ball and stay that way. How does anything alive just pop back?*

"You guys see that?" I said.

"I right?" the man said.

"He right?" the girl said.

"See what?"

"Am I right?"

"About what?"

"Father esquire."

I returned to my own car, reacquainting myself with the fact that I was sitting beside a strange, beautiful woman and an ex-con with tattooed fingers who claimed to be a mind reader. It was the only time I could think of I had been in my own car with two people whose names I didn't know, let alone one I thought might kill me, and one I felt like I might fall in love with if I looked at her one more time.

"Six for six," the man said.

"How'd you know that?" the girl said.

But it didn't take a mind reader to make an educated guess that someone who played tennis came from a family with money. And families with money, lots of them had a lawyer in the fold. Like mine. The guy was smart, but he was no mystic.

"And I'll tell you something else, since I'm on such a roll. You didn't think you were going to be the one driving this girl home." I let my eyes rise to the rearview. The pickup had stopped far back on the shoulder. In the backseat, the man leaned forward. "Yeah. Your buddies are the ones with the girlie luck. But look at you now."

"It's not like that," she said.

"Ah, but it is. Who was it that was supposed to be with her? Another tennis player. You play doubles?"

29

DOUBLES

I couldn't believe he knew what doubles was.

"Hit a nerve, huh?" Then he pointed his thumb at me and in a loud stage whisper said to the girl, "Still a virgin, too."

I frowned as if what he was saying were so ridiculous it didn't even require comment. But this guy was picking up on things. He was hitting too many of these shots. I could explain the lawyer guess for the most part but not the one that her father ran the museum. The day seemed hotter, the air through our open windows thicker. The girl pulled her towel tightly around her shoulders. I looked in the rearview, watching for the dog to reemerge.

"Know my trick?" the man said.

"What trick?" the girl said.

"How I read minds? Take my pretty picture. I'll tell you the truth."

The girl lifted a Polaroid camera from her bag.

"They make those in digital now," the man said.

She pushed a lever on the side of the metal case, and the enclosed device opened its old accordion skin. Then she turned. "OK. Tell me."

"First I'll read one more piece of your sweet little brain. You. Want. Me. Out of this car."

"Yeah. I. Do," she said.

"I know. And I'll tell you how I know. One, two"—he leaned forward, and the girl tensed, finger on the button—"because I'm a *mind* reader."

The man yelped in high laughter, and the flash filled the car, its power diffused by the sunlight, a small, white blink followed by a whir. Film emerged from the camera's mouth. Without reaction, the girl carefully plucked the photo and produced a ballpoint pen from her bag. I watched her write onto the white space at the bottom: I AM A MIND READER.

A Sinclair gas station appeared on my right, just off the exit. I came off the ramp and passed a concrete dinosaur in the lot, where tall, thin weeds rose from cracks like we had rolled onto the plane of a mangy asphalt scalp. There was one pump and no cars. The pump was so old, it read the price in plastic digits that spun behind a glass façade. I stopped in the small parallelogram of shade from the hanger and pulled a lever beneath the dash. The cover on the gas tank released with a metallic *boing*.

"Mind reader alert: You're thinking you're going to get rid of me and then go home and make out," he said. "You're both thinking that exact thing."

"We're not going anywhere," I said, laughing awkwardly as I got out of the car. He'd said exactly what I had been thinking. I took the hose from the antique pump and started to fill the Dart. The man stepped out of the car and started across the lot. He swung open the door to the convenience store so hard that it hit the side of the building. The glass shattered, falling into countless shards at his feet. He kept his arm high above his head, as if he had just thrown a handful of confetti into the breeze. I turned to the girl. She was playing air drums to the radio. The holster at the end of the hose jumped in my hand, a trickle overflowing the tank. "Hey!" I said.

She leaned out the window and said, "What?"

"Turn the car off!"

She waved her hand at the dash as if it should be forgotten. "Let's go."

The pump predated any technology that allowed you to pay. I turned towards the store. Inside, the man stood on his toes at the counter, leaning across it. He held the teenage teller's hair in his fist and slammed her face onto the counter. He raised her head and did it again. I turned. The girl in my car had turned back to her bag, where she was searching for something. I couldn't believe what I was seeing. I felt isolated by my senses. I got back into the car.

"You pay?" she said, putting on a pair of large sunglasses from the bag. She turned to look back as we rolled into the street. Already we had gone too far for her to see anything.

"Hey, you pay back there?"

"We needed to go."

Out of the corner of my eye, one foot, its toenails painted in chipped red, settled into the sun on my dash. I was afraid that if I told her what had just happened, it would ruin whatever good thing we had going on. Again we let the wind take over the car. It was soothing, knowing that not only did we not need to speak, but that she could not, in fact, even really hear me if I tried.

We took 54 into Chapel Hill, passing the tennis center to our left as we came to the bottom of the hill. She directed me to Rogerson Drive, a small road of cottages built in the 1940s for GI Bill students. We stopped at a small, yellow house with a red Nissan pickup truck in the driveway. She invited me in to dry off. One wall in her living room featured a series of Polaroids of her face in different expressions, the emotions written onto the white space. JOY (AT CHRISTMAS PRESENT). REGRET (DRUNK EMAIL TO JOEL). PAIN (ACTUAL PHYSICAL PAIN—INGROWN TOENAIL). REALLY FUNNY (AMERICA'S FUNNIEST HOME VIDEOS). NOT FUNNY AT ALL (BUT NICE PERSON TOLD THE JOKE—ALLISON). Another had a photo of the same dogwood in different shades of light and weather. In one photo snow hung heavy on its narrow branches, miniature icicles frozen in mid-drip hanging off of buds. In another, a colorful HAPPY BIRTHDAY sign hung draped across the branches. The sun rose through blossoms in one. Another was almost completely dark. Each had the date written on it. The television flickered silent on the evening news. Closed captions ran across the bottom.

She said, "I leave this on for Chewy."

"You really hard of hearing?" I said, looking for a pet.

"I'm deaf in one ear, part of the way in the other."

"How'd it happen?"

She shrugged, wiping the dust off the top of the TV with her fingertip. I thought about what the man had said about her being into me.

In the past, very few times in the past, girls had told me that friends of theirs liked me, that someone had a crush, that I should talk to so-and-so more. I know that part of it was self-defense, that I would rather not set myself up for failure, but I always thought, *Let them come to me*. If they like me, they'll talk. They never did, though. But this time, even though the words were from the mouth of a violent ex-con mind reader who was surely now running through some field, trailing dollar bills and Funyuns wrappers, fleeing the law and convenience store destruction in his wake, there was something there that I believed. I decided to act, whatever the chance. This one I wouldn't let get away.

"Take a photo of my teeth," I said.

"You gonna tell me the truth?"

"About what?"

"Tell me who sent you to talk to me."

"You're the one who spoke to me."

"Was it the Asian guy?"

"You believe that stuff?"

"Or was it the naked fool?"

I put my hands into the air like what she had said was ridiculous.

"That Chewy?" I said.

"Don't try to change the subject."

A dog door in the kitchen took up a good third of the regular door itself. The plastic flap was dirty and worn, and the edges of the opening were rough and widened by use. Through the back window I saw a sheepdog standing in the middle of the lawn, growling at a dirty German shepherd.

The girl followed my gaze and said, "Shit."

"That's the dog from the highway."

She opened the door. "Chewy, come here."

"Hey," I said, passing the girl and stepping into the lawn. "Hey!"

The German shepherd turned to me, teeth bared, and took a step back. It was like he had followed me there. Maybe my presence was enough. Animals sometimes responded to me in ways unusual to other humans. I thought it was my height. They must have thought I was a subspecies, an unknown quantity.

"Get!"

But the dog lunged. His lips curled enough that the damp, hidden flesh on their underside popped out, glistening with viscous goo. He snapped, like some lever had been thrown, a mechanical function meant to break and tear. His fans from the pickup truck would have run, screaming in terror. I swung away with the towel that I had been drying myself off with, and his teeth closed on the white terry cloth. It was the same motion as a swinging backhand volley. I was trained to respond to this. The towel lifted into the air on my follow-through, and the dog rose with it, growling and dangling below. I let the whole dog-towel unit swing full to my other side, then let go. The beast and towel flew over the low picket fence. The dog landed on his side in the grass and, just like he had on the shoulder of the highway, popped back up and ran.

Inside, Chewy lapped water from a bowl in the kitchen, splashing it across the fur on his face. His eyes were completely covered by wet hair. The girl lifted her camera from the table and tucked a red ballpoint pen into her ponytail. It stood erect like a plastic horn.

She said, "I have to have a record of the guy who saved Chewy."

She put the camera to her eye. I smiled.

"But when I take it," she said, "tell me what that guy did back there."

"Where?"

"Don't lie to me."

I sighed and said, "OK. He broke the glass door, then slammed the girl's face at the register into the counter."

She lowered the camera. "What?"

"I'm serious."

"No. I mean, I didn't hear you."

"He broke the glass door, then slammed the girl's face into the counter. The girl at the register."

"That's what's on TV," she said.

"What do you mean?"

I followed her gaze to the television. It was as if some psychic cloud had descended on my life, because there, on the silent evening news, a grainy black-and-white security camera video showed the man from my car doing exactly what I had just described.

"Holy shit!" The sound was still off, and I was too consumed with the image to see the captions. "What did they say?" I said, stepping closer to the TV. I couldn't find the volume on the set.

"Why didn't you tell me?"

By the time I found the volume, the segment had ended.

"Hey, weirdo. Why didn't you tell me?"

I kept turning it up. "What'd they say?"

"You saw him do that?"

"Did you hear what they said?"

"I bet he was from that jail."

"He was."

"He say that?"

"Yeah. Right when we drove by the sign."

"I didn't hear him."

"Well."

"So you knew."

"I knew once he told me."

"What?"

"I knew once he told me."

"And you didn't tell me."

"I thought you heard him."

She shook her head. "You didn't freak out?"

I shrugged, thrilled that she thought that it was information I took in stride. She looked at Chewy for a moment and seemed to take it in. "He would have killed us." She handed me the camera.

"Here," she said. "No, here. Don't just hold it."

I held it higher and looked at it, then back at her.

"No," she said. "Take my *picture*."

The small crosshairs in the viewfinder traversed her narrow nose, the sharp angles of her cheekbones, the bottom lip that protruded just a little further than her top. Her golden hair was like a dark canvas wiped free of paint, the white of the surface glowing through. She raised her eyebrows as if to ask if I was ready. I put my finger on the button. The room exploded with light. She took the pen from her hair and wrote onto the bottom of the developing photo, HAPPY (ABOUT MEETING THIS TALL GUY).

In the years since, Anne continued with the photos. I was always nervous around the camera. She would look at me through the viewfinder and ask me to tell her things that I'd never told a soul. I'd say, "I forgot to take out the trash last week." Flash. "I called a ball wide that I knew was in." Flash. "I read some of Kaz's email." Flash. She then would hand me the camera and tell me things I couldn't believe she would admit. That she had dreamt of having sex with my mother. Flash. That she had walked in on her father and cousin smoking marijuana together. Flash. After each she would look at the photo, ignoring the sudden truth in the room, and write the revelation at the bottom. I HIT A DOG BUT DIDN'T STOP 3/19/03.

Polaroid film is not cheap. It comes out to basically a dollar a photo. We had so many thousands of Polaroids around the house that I tried not to do the simple math. I learned that, when she asked me if I liked a photo, the worse it was the more I'd better say it was good. If I ever told her that I liked the photographs that actually looked good she would just roll her eyes and sigh.

We married thirteen months after we met, eight years ago. Right away, Anne wanted babies. I agreed in terror and resignation, then spent the next six and a half years trying to conceive in frantic sessions between international flights. For years I'd been terrified of getting anyone pregnant—not that I'd had much of a chance to—but suddenly it was the last thing I could do. She said I didn't want it. I went to the doctor of my own volition, the first time I had ever done that for anything other than an injury. He told me they needed to do further tests. I never took more tests. I never told Anne I'd even gone. She was against medical intervention. If it was meant to happen, it would, she said.

I took Anne to Forest Hills with me last year, like always. We stayed at Manny and Katie's. During a discussion of politics, Katie mentioned that she had had two abortions. In bed that night, looking away from me on her side of the bed, Anne sobbed for hours. Three weeks later she called me in Paris to tell me she was pregnant. I thought how funny it was how these things work. I was so glad I'd never mentioned the doctor. The best part was simply how happy Anne had suddenly become.

Every morning during her pregnancy, she attached her camera to the top of a small tripod and stood at the end of our hallway, in front of the white closet door, and pushed a button at the end of a wire. Her body—always so thin, hip bones protruding—was becoming something she had always desired—a thing with curves, a place brimming with life. She wanted it all on film, every step. In the photos, she rarely looked at the camera, just to the side, as if she were in a scientific study. When I returned between tournaments, she would show me the daily growth of her stomach, frame by frame. Each day, her stomach grew closer to the closet doorknob, like a sentence slowly writing itself up to a period. By January, when I was home for two weeks before the Australian, the sentence was almost completed.

One night, I sat in the living room, reading the paper for the first time in weeks while Anne washed dishes in the kitchen.

"There ice in the trays?" she called out.

"Yeah, I think."

"Hey, Slow, there ice in the trays?"

I sighed, stood, and set the paper down.

"Yeah," I said, stepping into the kitchen. "I said yes."

"Will you look?"

"Why do you need ice now?"

"I might want some after the dishes."

I opened the freezer. There was no ice. I filled three trays and put them back in.

"It won't be frozen by the time you finish," I said.

"I think so, yeah."

"No," I said, raising my voice. "I said, *it won't be frozen.*"

She kept placing dishes on the rack, washing, placing. Finally, when she saw that I was still in the room, she said, "What?"

"The ice is *not* going to be frozen," I said. "It's not even going to be close."

She shut off the water and turned, her stomach suddenly huge and tight before her as she dried her hands on the top of it.

"What?"

Even though she was looking right at me, from only feet away, and the water was off, I raised my voice. "I said the ice isn't going to be frozen!"

She turned back to the sink in silence.

I looked at the words in the morning paper again until I heard Anne on the front stoop. Our windows were open at all times, on days when it was so cold morning condensation would freeze on the inside of the panes. Anne felt strongly about the circulation of air. I opened the door. A blast of cold air blew in hard against my flesh, and I thought how nice the Australian summer was going to be. It was only days away. Anne was on the top step, her back to me.

"Let's go for a ride," I said.

It was all I could think of that might cut the tension. The Dart was our emotional normalizer, an eraser of marital stress. I had begun to learn how to repair it. I felt like the work I put into it was work into relationship stability. That morning, I'd fixed the radio and installed a new brake pedal. The brake pedal was easy. You just detach the foot plate with a pin, lead a little piston into the hydraulic lever, and put the pin back in. What I was most excited about was the radio. It was an easy fix; the speaker connections were just corroded. I hadn't told Anne. The radio was going to be a surprise.

She followed me across the mossy lawn like a pregnant sleep-walker, silent and mysterious and removed. We drove through our neighborhood in silence, slowly, running low in third gear. I'd set the idle high for the cold weather, and at stop signs we pittered loudly in the darkness like a huge boiling vat. I was saving the radio until University Lake. We slowly approached 15-501. This was one of the local roads rendered unrecognizable with civic growth. Headlights flew by in expanded lanes at speeds that were unvisited on my speed-ometer. I downshifted and stepped on the new brake pedal. But my foot couldn't find it. I looked down and in the dim light saw the pedal lying on the floor. I didn't panic, just began to ease the emergency brake up. I don't think Anne even noticed something was wrong. For a brief moment, as we rolled into the intersection, I still thought we were going to be fine. Then we jerked to the right, and the sound of crunching metal filled the car as a red mass exploded through the windshield.

A headlight, still lit, was suddenly where Anne's belly had been. Handlebars reached at odd angles around her head. Somehow the radio was now on, and Bob Seger was singing "Night Moves." Cars screeched. A Hummer slid off the road and shuddered to a stop in a ditch. I opened my door. A man kneeled on the pavement, holding his shoulder. He pulled off a gleaming black helmet. "I'm fine!" he said, almost cheerfully. "I'm fine!" A motorcycle lay on the hood of my car, its back wheel spinning slowly in midair.

I opened Anne's door and pushed the bike away from her. Freed from her flesh, the headlight now flooded the car with light. The skin on Anne's forehead had been wiped aside like wet dough. Her dress was molded around shapes I did not understand, red seeping through the fabric like a paper towel placed atop spilled wine. A falsetto moan came from my mouth, a sound I had never before made. It was animal.

"What happened?" Anne said.

I sang that eerie note and held her, my face on her shoulder. I could feel the blood pumping out of her and onto my arms. I couldn't speak. I just moaned. She leaned her head onto mine as Bob Seger sang about working on his night moves in the sweet sweet summertime.

At University Hospital I waited for news on our baby, but it never came. I deduced that it was gone over a night of slow, silent logic. I never learned the sex. I never even asked. I was too scared that I might be charged with killing it. At first the surgeon said Anne would regain consciousness, that there was brain trauma but no permanent damage. Their biggest concern was a piece of spring from the front seat that had lodged itself in her spine.

After that first night in the hospital, I packed a bag with three changes of Anne's clothes, her bathrobe, a toothbrush, a hairbrush, and her camera. But when that first day—filled with fluorescent-lit faces puffed with fear and ballpoint pens tearing into damp forms with nibs that wouldn't flow—neared a close, I took the camera out of her canvas bag and shot her myself. There was no longer a baby inside that skin, but I knew that Anne would want the photo. It was another opportunity to watch her body transform, this a newer stage, a movement apart and away. She would appreciate my filling the brief window of time that she couldn't. Then two days passed, then five, then a week and a half. I forgot about the spring. Comas existed only on *General Hospital*. I didn't know anyone who even knew anyone who had been in one. But now Anne was in what the doctor called a coma. I called it a strung out state of living death, of waiting, of beeping and whirring and sponges. But still I continued to shoot. After a week I couldn't imagine stopping. The accumulating frames made me feel like I was in control of a situation that was uncontrollable. As long as I photographed Anne every day, nothing could happen—not even a change of the sheets—that I didn't know about. During the initial transformation, the changes were dramatic. Weight loss and a tightening of features combined with the healing of wounds and the disappearance of bruising. Then, after about five weeks, she leveled off. The only change over dozens of photos was a rotation in bedding, in pillowcases, in different colored tubes into her nose and mouth. Otherwise the photos looked the same. They all looked like someone who had at one point been my wife, had once been alive, had once kissed me and started to cry because she was afraid I wouldn't love her as much once the baby was born.

4

ANNE BEGAN TO appear. The faint outline of her head darkened first from the Polaroid murk, then a glistening spot on her withered bottom lip wet with saliva and salve shone out from the hardening form. Turquoise bed sheets rose in the bottom of the frame like a small body of water lapping up at her chin. Before the color could fully develop I wrote the date on the bottom and slid it into the envelope.

"You hear me, girl?" Manny said, waving a hand in front of Anne's face.

I placed my fingers around her wrist just to see how easy it would be. Her pulse drummed hidden and buried within. It was the one magic trick of life I could still always locate.

"You think if she wakes up, she's going to have amnesia?" Manny said.

"Why would she have amnesia?"

"Hey, girl."

"Why would she have amnesia?"

"She doesn't deserve this place," Manny said. "Let's get her out of here." He swung his arms around her face. "Hey," he said, "I know you hear me." After a few moments he gave up and said, sighing, "My cousin works here."

"Who?"

"You know Yellow Dog?"

I knew Yellow Dog. He had a short blond moustache and spiked blond hair and wore a hemp choker necklace with beads. When he introduced himself to me, he said, "Yellow Dog is un*usual*." I hadn't seen him in years.

"I'm gonna go find him," Manny said.

"What's he do?"

"Anesthesiologist," Manny said. "I know. Right?"

After he left I looked down at Anne. The slackness in her face had rendered her a distant relative of herself. Her lips had thinned and tightened around her teeth. Her hair was clumped in grease. Sudden complex topography appeared where bone met bone. Sometimes I was convinced that she could wake up if she wanted. I looked around the room, as if someone might have secretly entered. It was still dark and silent and empty. I poked Anne in the cheek. My finger pressed against the edge of a molar.

"Hey," I whispered and tapped her on the forehead.

I turned to the door, making sure no one was looking through the small square of wire-hatched glass. It was blank, a glowing box of fluorescence. I turned back to Anne, pinched her left eyelid, and pulled it open. The pale blue eyeball beneath stared ahead at nothing. So many times in the past it had gazed at me through viewfinders, sent me into spasms of nerves and thrill and love. It was her most vital organ. If anything was going to spring to life first, this would be it. It was one of the only parts of her body I had never touched. I placed my index finger on it and pressed. The cool surface gave just lightly under pressure. I stopped in terror and took my finger away. My wife's blue eye looked back at nothing, motionless and cold and still under my hovering fingertip.

5

THE DASHBOARD HELD our knees close to our chests. The dog moved from my lap to a narrow space behind the seats. The highways held so many shared memories. We used to drive this route endlessly, up and back through satellites and challengers. In college too, this was our interstate, an artery through the ACC. Up I-85 to I-95, into Virginia, over bilane stretches, north and southbound separated by a dark stretch of woods. We reached the northernmost Bojangles in America. I couldn't remember who had ascertained this fact. It might not have even been true, but it was inarguable in our personal geography. We purchased a box of fried chicken with Combover's Visa.

Manny moved into the left lane and passed a cop.

"They respect you if you do that," he said, tossing a chicken wing into the widening space between the two cars. An Ennio Morricone score blared out of the tiny speakers.

"What's up with the whole cowboy thing?" I said.

"How'd you know about my cowboy thing?"

"You're wearing cowboy boots. There are horns on the front of the car. You're listening to Ennio Morricone."

"Slow!"

It was always something. Westerns were his new thing. The great American form. The strength of violence on screen. The epic storylines. "We should have never done away with the duel," he proclaimed. "Conflict resolution!"

My mind kept drifting back to tennis. In southern Virginia we passed a black man standing alone on a hill at the edge of the interstate, at the far end of a motel parking lot. He was wearing yellow rubber gloves that reached to his elbows, and a rolled white towel was wrapped around his neck. He was just standing there, watching traffic. I thought, *That man would never play tennis. He probably thinks tennis is stupid.* It seemed the ultimate reproach to my previous life. I felt that whatever a black man with large yellow gloves at the edge of an interstate felt was unequivocally true. An endorsement of my retirement. But later Manny switched to talk radio, where a woman carried on about championship rose gardening. She said, "For gardeners, some of them, this is just competitive. For them, it's just like tennis." At the word, I started, as if she had mentioned a relative. *Tennis?* I thought. *That's mine!* I took offense. For me, I thought, tennis was not just competitive. For me, tennis was rose gardening.

North of DC, I filled the Fiat at a truck stop while Manny jogged in place beside the pump. The heels of his cowboy boots clopped in time on the oily asphalt.

"Legs like these," he said, "are just waiting to clot."

I swiped Combover's card.

Inside, Manny filled his arms with VHS Westerns from a discount bin. "Put these on Combover," he said, letting them tumble onto the counter. "It's business. These and pump 2. Got pornos? You want any pornos, Slow? Hey? Slow?"

When the Manhattan skyline rose through the New Jersey refinery towers, Manny perked up like he'd never seen it before. He pointed at the jagged, gray mass in the distance and said, "Slow!"

Even the dog turned.

Manny parked his Fiat on the west side on the lower level of a pier beside the *Intrepid*, the ancient old warship clanging under the footsteps of children high above.

"Two hundred dollars a month," he said, pulling into the space. "I need to get another Vanagon and live right *here*."

He held his hand out towards a Hudson filled with evening sunlight, and I thought he might be onto something. The smell of the water seemed exotic and familiar. The sun was unfiltered by the dense growth of my neighborhood. Here there was less humidity. If any mosquitoes were in the air, there was such a glut of humanity to choose from that they barely noticed my pale flesh. We walked north up Eleventh Avenue, through a throng of foreign tourists waiting to catch the next Circle Line.

We turned right on Fifty-second Street, an undistinguished block of five-story walk-ups all seemingly tilting to one side, antennaed water towers peeking from between ancient, crumbling cornices.

A young woman with fair skin sat on a stoop with a metal mixing bowl propped between her knees. She wore a low-cut shirt that revealed her small, freckled cleavage. Oversize red sunglasses rose as we approached. Manny's upper lip curled into a sneer. He said, "M'lady."

The woman smiled and said, "Hello."

"Yeah," Manny said, nodding.

"Who is your walking companion?"

She spoke in exact, clipped syllables, each with its own perfect place, delineated by abruptly cut consonants, soft, accent-free vowels. She sounded like a telephone recording come to life.

"It's my player. My Slow. My best friend."

"Paige," she said.

I held up my hand.

"You shy?" she said.

"He's a wild man," Manny said, slapping me on my back.

"Are you related?"

"Brothers-in-arms."

47

DOUBLES .....

"I'm not shy," I said.

"You live in the state of North Carolina as well?"

"Yeah," I said. "Where are you from?"

"New Orleans."

"Does everybody there talk like that?"

She laughed. "I'm trained in speech," she said, then waved her hand back and forth as if her answer was only so-so.

"Like ads?" I said. "You look familiar."

"People say I look like the screen actress Scarlett Johansson."

"He's heard all about you," Manny said. "What you peeling?"

"Quail eggs."

She held out a miniature egg, and Manny wrapped his giant lips around it. She held one to me. I softly pinched it between my fingers. It reminded me of Anne's eyeball. It was so delicate, this boiled nascent bird. I didn't want to chew it. But I put it in my mouth out of courtesy and held it there, rolling it across my tongue. As I did, my eyes met Paige's. She just kept looking at me. I swallowed it whole. When I finished, Paige smiled softly like we shared a secret.

In my memory, rooms opened upon rooms in Manny's apartment. There were corners where anything could be found. The walls read the subtle braille of decades of layered paint. Manny had built a trick bar, which swung open to reveal his freakishly long clothes hanging within a hidden chamber. There was even a backyard. I had spent months of my life there, months of my youth. Weeks without tournaments where I would wake late and not move, dreaming about the city outside. Once, walking home to the apartment one afternoon, coming from an Adidas storage space in Midtown, where'd I'd selected boxes of free clothing, I just started to laugh. I had stepped into a dream only to find that its ghostly, ridiculous landscape was real.

All of those times, Katie had been in the apartment, her elegance combining with Manny's slop to create a chamber of worn Oriental carpets, dusty photo albums of trips to North Africa, Greece. Pottery. Framed paintings. Large, beautiful books.

When I entered the apartment this time, the space had shrunk.

"Shit hole sweet shit hole," Manny said.

The living room held a small table, a blue love seat, and two plastic chairs. The walls were bare. The top of a miniature TV was piled with more VHS Westerns. In the corner was a Ouija board, which Manny folded into a box.

"Ain't she a peach?" he said, putting the Ouija board away. "You open to the spirit world?"

I had forgotten that the backyard was accessible only from the window. I looked out and saw it had been paved. The guest room was filled almost from wall to wall with a single mattress on the floor.

"Where's Katie living?"

"Who wants to die rich?" Manny said. "Know what I'm saying?"

I did not know.

"But where is she? Where's she staying?"

"Slow, you always did worry about her. But I'll get her back. Don't you worry." He peered into the guest room and sighed. "This is all yours, until my next client."

"Client?"

"Client, renter."

"Subletter?"

"Yeah. I find them on Craigslist. Just had some Columbia guy in here for two weeks, computer programming."

"For how much?"

"Nothing. Six hundred a week."

"How much you pay?"

"Eight hundred a month. Rent control." He watched me do the math. "I'm keeping it real."

"These guys know?"

"Slow, some of these guys, they're getting paid like a couple grand a week."

"Where's the Columbia guy?"

"He . . ." Manny shook his head. "He was great. Loved that guy, *loved* him. It was just, he just had this one problem. I mean, you tell me, Slow. Tell me. What's the one thing every apartment in New York has?"

"Roaches?"

"No. Ah, Slow, that's a good one, though. I mean this guy was from Kansas originally. They got, what, tornadoes like daily out there? Well, this motherfucker. I come home one day and he is standing on a chair. *Seriously.*"

"For what? Mice?"

"Well he says they were rats, but come on. I mean even if they are, I want them here. I mean, if you're a rat, you got as much right to live in this city as I do."

"So he left?"

"No, he asked me to do something about them. Said he found one in his bed."

"Jesus."

"Yeah," Manny said. He fished a frozen sausage out of the freezer. "He finally just lost it."

"So what'd you do?"

He held the sausage under hot water from the tap.

"Are you serious? About rats?" he said, shaking off the sausage. Then he yelled, "Rats! You hear me? I know you belong. We're all fucking rats!"

He set his food on the miniature table in the living room, then pressed play on a video camera wired to the television. He always had that camera with him, shooting workouts and matches, analyzing groundstrokes. He settled back into the love seat. I stood in the doorway and watched, expecting tennis. Instead, a grainy black-and-white video began to play of a naked man leaning over a naked woman, kissing her stomach. A huge grin spread across Manny's face.

"The hell is this?" I said.

"Ain't no shame in this."

I leaned in. "Who is that?"

He smiled wider.

On screen, Manny now stood up and said, "You want red or white?"

The woman said, "I don't care."

He laughed on screen. He laughed in the room. I squinted, the woman just thighs and stomach. Then she sat up. It was Katie. She looked anatomical. A body captured. Manny climbed on top of her. I watched between fingers. I thought of my own life in contrast and felt like I was a hundred years old. On screen Manny moaned like a bad actor. Katie moaned back. He turned up the volume and whispered, "Listen. Listen. I write good material."

Video Manny said, "You like that?" and Video Katie said, "Yeah." He said, "You like it when I do monkey-style?" She said, "Oh yeah."

"The hell are you saying?" I said.

"I don't know." He turned it up. "I write good material."

"She know you were taping?"

"No. Shhhh."

Video Katie said, "Oh Jesus. Oh Jesus." Her legs kicked the air, then her feet settled on either side of Manny's face.

He looked at me and nodded. "But she knew."

Video Katie said, "What did you do to them?"

"I did this," Video Manny said.

"What'd you say?"

"I said, 'You like it monkey-style?'"

"Say it."

"You like it monkey-style?"

"Yeah."

He barked like an ape. "Oh oh ah ah ah! You like that. You like the monkey-style?"

"Yeah!"

I said, "Why do you keep saying that?"

"I just made it up! Watch. She wants me to choke her."

She reached up and began to choke him.

"She's choking *you*," I said.

"I should have gone into porn, Slow."

"I don't think it's that hard to get into."

"No, it is," he laughed, breathlessly. "There was this one post on Craigslist . . ."

But he trailed off to watch himself flip Katie over. She finally said, "Now choke me."

"There it is," he said, pointing at the screen and nodding.

Manny fast-forwarded until the woman who had just fed me a quail egg was standing before us, naked on the television, flossing her teeth. The view was partially blocked by cloth, clearly a camouflage, of which Paige was oblivious. She was thin in places that I thought she would be full, round in others, a revelation from what I had encountered on the street.

"*Konichiwa*, bitches," Manny said. I turned to him in shock. He held his cell phone onto the side of his face as the video played on. He raised his eyebrows and pointed at the phone, as if it were of great secret importance. I knew who it was. "Kaz, no. Listen," he said. "Listen. You need to meet me at the *secret place*. OK. You don't? OK. I'll tell you where it is."

The buzzer sounded, and Manny motioned to it, too busy with the phone to bother. I pressed ENTER. Steps sounded down the hallway, and he just held the phone to his ear and nodded. There was a knock at the door, and Manny motioned towards it with his hand, as if I should open it. I made no move, though, unsure if he was really serious about not shutting off the tape first. As I waited, the door opened on its own, and Paige stepped through, holding a lit cigarette in one hand while feeding herself a peeled quail egg in the other. I stood before her in the narrow hallway and turned to Manny in desperation. He looked up, then dropped to the floor. His cell phone skidded across the hardwood. He yanked the connecting cables from the back of the camera. The television went blank as Paige stepped around me.

"What were you watching?" she said.

Manny looked up from his knees. Kaz's voice squeaked tiny from the cell phone. "Hello? Hello?" But Manny said nothing, just grinned up at Paige.

"You were watching me, weren't you?"

He opened his mouth in mock amazement. Paige turned to me.

"Did you just see me naked?" she said.

I looked at Manny, but he kept his eyes on her.

"You did," she said. She took a drag from the cigarette, then blew a mouthful of smoke into my face. "I want to see it."

As the smoke blew past my ears, Manny slowly stood up, holding his hands in front of him. She blew more smoke at him. It curled around his long, thin fingers.

"If you don't show me, I'm going to put this out on your chest," she said. "I swear to fucking God."

"Why am I annoying you?" Manny said.

"What?"

"It just seems like lately I've been annoying you."

"You have been."

"What is it?"

"You're annoying."

"You love me," he said and reached for her. She let him grab her around the waist, but held her head away from him. Then she raised the cigarette to his face and said, "You tell me what you were watching, or I swear to God I'm going to put this out on your nose."

I believed, 100 percent, that she would do exactly that.

Then she turned and asked me again. "You just see me naked?"

"No," I said. I knew I wasn't convincing. I had to give her something, or I was going to crack. "But I might have just seen *somebody* naked."

"Katie?" Paige said, and Manny smiled his huge smile.

Paige placed her cigarette back into her mouth, and Manny kissed her on the cheek. She walked into the kitchen, and Manny looked at me in relief. Static flickered on the television, buzzing in the corner. I missed this crazy logic. Being here with Manny made me feel sane for the first time in months. I thought, There is no growing up, no childhood and then adulthood. Not for us. There are just constants, traits that harden. Patterns that must repeat. Allegiances. To my wife, to Kaz, and to Manny, who was now drinking champagne with a woman whom I had known for under an hour and whom I had already seen naked. I was confident that these lines were messy and thrilling but permanent. I let Paige pour me a glass.

Manny raised his drink into the air.

"Frankenfurter!" he said. It made no sense. It was a remnant of some locker room joke from a European challenger tournament in 1999. I couldn't even remember what it was supposed to mean. But that didn't matter. What mattered was that it was ours, a benchmark in our shared history.

"Frankenfurter," I said and drank.

6

I STOOD BEFORE an unlit glass storefront with a dusty mannequin in the window. In white hand-painted lettering, a crooked green sign hung by twine around the mannequin neck read DRY CLEANING $2 A SHIRT. Heavy velvet curtains blocked the view of the rest of the shop.

"This is it," Manny said.

"This is what?"

"This is the secret place."

I looked back at the mannequin. "In there?"

"It's secret."

Kaz finally appeared under a streetlamp in a dark blue Adidas workout suit, his hair tied into a short, greasy ponytail. He had a thin beard. As he neared, I could already see that his fingernails were long. It was the telltale growth of a winning streak. When he was winning, he wouldn't shave or cut his hair. He kept a diary of everything he ate and did on a day of tournament play so that, if it worked, he could re-create that exact day again when needed. As his partner, I was caught up in this cycle. After six years of winning, our routines at Forest Hills were concrete. Where we ate, when we ate, how we slept, whom we saw. Other tournament routines could shift dramatically from year to year, changing with different results. But at Forest Hills the routines were always the same, the results always victory.

He looked up and stopped walking.

"What are you doing?" he said. Traces of his Japanese childhood still lingered in his wide vowels.

"Manny got me."

Kaz looked at Manny in confusion.

"Got you what?"

I looked at Manny.

"You two can't be apart," Manny said. "Get Slow out there with you."

"With me for what?" Kaz said.

My face warmed with blush.

"I know you need him for all your voodoo shit."

"He can't play," Kaz said.

"Manny," I said.

"Just work out. Get things going."

Kaz laughed nervously, and that's when I knew what this was. Kaz hadn't said anything about my coming back. This was about Manny. No one else wanted his fake coaching. For us, we knew that wasn't what he was good for. He was a hitting partner, a stringer, and a booker of hotels, but he was more than that. He was our entertainment and our comfort. I had rarely thought about the fact that he also needed us. But now, as he stared at us with that sheepish grin, I thought about the fact that he was unemployed. This was his parent trap. He wanted his bosses to reunite. He wanted his job back.

Kaz hugged me. I smelled his deep onion body odor, snorted in disgust, and said, "Guess you've been winning."

So much time together had rendered our relationship stiff in surprising ways. Manners and silences maintained sanity after years of shared space and fortune. The dim light from a streetlamp on the corner glistened on Kaz's greasy eyelids, low over his thin, almond eyes. Young men and women in tight jeans and tighter T-shirts with floppy hats and messenger bags passed us on the sidewalk, looking sidelong at me and Kaz holding each other, gazing into each other's eyes.

"Come on, kids," Manny said. He opened the door to the secret place and beckoned us into the dark.

Kaz and I had been partners for twenty-three years. His family lived in Midway, the ghetto of Chapel Hill, a neighborhood less than two square miles located adjacent to some of the most expensive real estate in the state. The neighborhood was occupied with genera-tions of black families whom the rest of Chapel Hill either ignored or arrested. His mother was Japanese, but his father was one of a long line of black Midway residents and had been born in a house three blocks from where they now lived. He had been stationed as an air force mechanic in South Korea in the late '70s, and when he returned, he came with Kaz and his mother, Sue.

For years, Sue had barely spoken a word of English, but when we were in sixth grade she opened Sue-nami, a sushi restaurant off Highway 54. It was in a strip mall in what used to be an old gun shop, and the walls were hung with wallpaper made from large-scale photographs of life-size trees. It was engineered to produce the illusion that you had entered a clearing in a forest. When we were in high school, after practice, we would go to Sue-nami and Sue would bring us wooden boats filled with sushi. Afterwards we would lie on the blue carpet and she would massage us by walking across our backs, one foot on each of us. I envisioned toxins releas-ing with each tiny step, knots untying in my tight shoulders. Kaz and I would sometimes end up facing each other on the floor, side by side, laughing and grunting and moaning as she made her way across shoulders tightened from hundreds of serves. I never knew if it was a Japanese tradition or not. For all I knew, it could have been Sue's invention. My family did not attend church, but for me this was prayer. It was ritual. It was otherworldly and relaxing and transporting.

Sue's husband was a welder who dropped a bundle of rebar on his left foot and crushed it. It was amputated when Kaz was five. Part of his rehabilitation included exercise on the cheapest prosthetic I had ever seen, just an oblong slab of jiggling rubber that he kept shoed with a black velcro Reebok. There was a tennis court near Midway at an apartment complex called Millcreek, which was occupied almost entirely by undergraduates so well-to-do that they didn't need to live in dorms, they could live in a complex with its own well-maintained tennis court that none of them ever used. Or if they did use the court, they were too scared to try when the one-footed black man with bloodshot eyes was on it hitting muddy tennis balls to a five-year-old half-Japanese kid. My older cousin lived in Millcreek at the time. I don't remember when I first met Kaz, but I do remember playing tennis with him there while his father sat in the shade of a pine tree at the farthest edge of the court and smoked a menthol Kool.

By twelve we were ranked ninth in the country for doubles. Individually we rotated in and out of the top 15. By high school we had already been partners for almost a decade. Sometimes when Kaz left a message on my answering machine, I mistook him for myself— on my *own phone*. On VH1 a few weeks ago, Keith Richards had said that the Rolling Stones weren't a band anymore; they were now a single musician. I thought, *That's how it is with Kaz.*

During our troubles getting pregnant, Anne told me that she resented the fact that every time she ovulated I was in a hotel room with Kaz. I *was* always in a hotel room with Kaz, or a locker room, or a tennis court. I was everywhere with Kaz. I always had been.

Manny led us into a short, dark hallway, no larger than a closet, and the door swung shut behind us. The space was draped in thick velvet curtains, one of which Manny parted to reveal a narrow room lit only by candles. A bar stood in the middle against the left wall. Six or seven booths and a few chairs at the bar were the only seating options. At the end of the room, on a stage no larger than my bed, stood a large-breasted woman in a red dress beside a suited man playing the vibraphone. The woman sang softly in Spanish.

"She saying, hombre?" Manny said. Kaz spoke Spanish but did not answer. I did not, but I'd taken enough Spanish classes in middle school to know this one. *Love, your heart is on fire. Love, my heart is on fire. I die. I die.* She repeated herself in drawn-out notes, stretching the melody. I wondered if Kaz didn't translate because of me.

Manny ordered three tall, thin glasses topped with thick foam.

"There's egg in these," he said, sliding one to Kaz. "They make some crazy shit."

"There alcohol in it?" Kaz said.

"You need to chill."

"I have to play tomorrow."

Manny lifted his glass. Kaz tentatively sipped at the foam. I followed his lead. Within minutes, our collective mood began to change. Manny told the story of his threesome. Kaz leaned in, listening intently.

"I don't believe it," he said.

"Ask her yourself," Manny said. "She's coming tomorrow."

I had not felt so relaxed in months. I gave Combover's Visa to Manny, and he went to the bar for more.

Kaz and I watched the woman in red. The Spanish was now beyond my grasp. The music was ethereal and hard to follow. Circular melodies rose above wavering notes from the vibraphone. I felt like I had entered a spell.

"Manny's a nut job," Kaz said.

"This afternoon he showed me a sex tape."

"He showed me one, too," Kaz said.

We let that sit.

"How are you?" Kaz said.

"Good."

"Pictures?"

"Every day."

"They say . . . ?"

I shook my head. "It's just waiting."

"Zip it zip it zip it," Manny said, returning from the bar. "Let's see if those girls will dance."

He pushed more frothy glasses into our hands and pointed to the bar. Two Indian women sat on the tall stools, both wearing long orange dresses that glimmered metallically in the soft light. They smoked cigarettes and scowled at each other, shaking their heads. They were older than us and seemed intent on a calm evening of disgust at whatever it was they were discussing. But Manny was not deterred. He spread his huge lips into that grin and held his arms open wide. He said, "Ladies!" then he put an arm on the back of each and leaned in. I don't know what he said next, but it worked. The women stood, looking at each other in mild surprise, as if they had both been lifted into the air by some unseen force. Manny started to dance, and then we all were—Kaz with one of the women in his arms, Manny with the other, and I by myself. I hated dancing, but I had never wanted to dance so much in my life. I invented a dance. It was called the groundstroke. I hit a forehand winner, then a backhand winner. Forehand winner, slice. Forehand winner, backhand winner. Forehand winner, slice. I tossed an invisible ball and served it directly to Kaz, who returned it across the bar. Manny was licking the face of his partner. I started to feel like I might fall. I held myself against the bar and laughed, pointing at Manny licking the Indian woman.

"Do that!" I yelled. "Do that!"

I sat on the damp floor. Manny ran towards me. I closed my eyes and laughed. I threw an invisible beanbag through the air and yelled, "Cornhole!" but the sound didn't come out. I was amazed at the silence.

"Cornhole! Cornhole! Cornhole!"

7

AFTER THE ACCIDENT, friends did not fly in for support. The ones that were already in town stayed away. People would drop off food, silently leaving it on my doorstep even when I was home, sitting ten feet away on the couch.

Kaz, though. The day after the accident, he moved into my guest room.

That night he took me to Sue-nami. In the entryway hung photos of the two of us at Wimbledon, the French Open, at Forest Hills. Playing at Ephesus Park at age nine. One of Kaz's old racquets hung behind the register, a wooden Wilson with its press clamped on. The wallpaper of trees had faded to a dull yellow, the vast forest finally now in autumn. His mother hugged me and led us to a table built around a huge central range. I could tell she was nervous, unsure of what to say. A miniature fishing boat filled with sushi arrived, rolls I would never be able to identify. By myself, I was helpless in a sushi restaurant. I had been too spoiled for years, riches of raw fish delivered to me by women who smiled and nodded enthusiastically. We ate it all and more. We drank massive amounts of sake and laughed at a waitress who had a piece of dried seaweed stuck to her rear end. It seemed impossible that one piece of seaweed could hang on for that long. I felt like it was the first funny thing I'd seen in weeks.

After the meal, Kaz's mother directed us to lie on the floor. There was only one other couple dining. She didn't care what they thought.

We positioned ourselves prostrate on our stuffed stomachs. Kaz's mother was just a little thing, not even five feet tall. She took the shoes off her miniature feet and then stepped onto us, one foot apiece. Then she began to walk in small steps, up and down our backs, strategically placing each foot on the right muscles.

"It make you digest," she said. The same explanation she had intoned for years.

After dark that night, I got out of bed to adjust the AC. In the hallway I heard a pulsing gasp from behind the closed door of the guest room. I leaned towards the sound. It was Kaz. I was scared of what I was hearing. But still I listened. It was sobbing.

The next day Kaz bought plywood, two-by-fours, and power tools. He must have spent hundreds of dollars on those tools. They're still in my closet, used only that one afternoon.

When he took me outside he held out his arms. On either side of my backyard stood a ramp of wood at a low angle off the ground. Each had a hole cut near its high point.

"Cornhole," he said.

"Excuse me?"

Red and black beanbags filled a white milk crate. Kaz lifted two and threw. The first hit the board with a thud and slid off the end, but the second arced high and dropped straight through the hole. He turned and said, "Cornhole."

I soon began to worry that my neighbors would complain. For days, the thump of beanbags on wood was constant. One night we played so long that Kaz eventually drove to Wal-Mart and bought a bag of glowsticks, which he placed inside the holes and along the edges of the boards so that we could continue into the darkness. My yard looked like it had grown two miniature alien landing strips.

I developed a highly effective technique involving a low bend and release. One Sunday we were eating breakfast at Dip's, a family soul food restaurant, and I said, "My butt is so sore from cornhole." My butt really was sore. The diners around us turned, and I felt a strange and guilty joy, like I was playing hooky. That I shouldn't be having fun.

"Let's get our tickets," Kaz said.

It was two days before Delray Beach. He'd been with me for almost two weeks by then. We were so conditioned to fly one-way internationally on a few hours' notice that it was the only travel that made sense.

I said, "I need to think about it."

"We have to move."

"Give me another day."

"We have to leave."

"I gotta stay."

"For what?"

"I don't know!"

He looked around the crowded dining room, then sighed and stared into his grits.

"You don't have to wait for me," I said.

It's not hard to find a doubles partner on short notice. As long as you get there in time and make the rankings cutoff, you can show up and just put your name on the sign-up form and see who else comes in. But Kaz didn't have to resort to that. He got on the phone and had a replacement within the hour. Gentleman John Maxwell, who stood six-two and had legs that looked swollen with thick tendon and muscle. John was known for immaculate and obsessive control. He bullied partners into agonizing practice times, stretched workouts too long, arranged endless court schedules around his convenience. When he served, it sounded like a baseball being hit. He was top 50.

Kaz kept asking, "Are you sure?"

"Just go," I said.

This was the start of my sleeping late and some of that other stuff. What I should have done is filed for my protective ranking immediately, because every week you don't play, you lose more points. But I kept planning to return in a week or two. By the time I finally filed, I had lost almost a third of my points and was 112th in the world.

I almost never had the urge to play. Intricacies of brands of grip, changes in ball velocity on different surfaces, altitudes, strategies honed over years were now useless. There was a feeling of deadweight and waste.

For a few days after Kaz left I played cornhole by myself. One afternoon I threw cornhole on all four bags. Four cornholes was impossible. The toss is thirty feet long, and the hole is only six inches wide. When the fourth bag passed into that small, magical void, I fell to my knees in my backyard and screamed up at the trees like I had just won Wimbledon.

8

I OPENED MY eyes to the back of Manny's couch. My head felt like it had been filled with cotton. I knocked over a cup of water on the floor as I swung my legs around and sat.

"That my little Slow?" Manny called, water puddling around my clammy heels.

The smell of eggs filtered through the cotton in my head, and I walked slowly towards the kitchen, where Manny stood in limp white underwear pulled high above his navel, like a skeleton in a loincloth frying eggs.

"Jesus," I said, rubbing my eyes. "I feel like I got drugged."

"That's because I drugged you."

Manny flipped the eggs onto a plate.

"Seriously."

Manny turned and said, "No, I'm serious too. I drugged you."

I remembered nothing past cornhole.

"I gobstopped you," Manny said.

"I'm sorry?"

"GHB. Yellow Dog came to play."

"GHB?"

He set a plate of eggs and toast in front of me, like a nurse tending the sick. "These are for you."

"You serious?"

"You guys needed to relax."

"You can't drug us."

"Those eggs is getting cold, Slow."

The idea that I had been drugged by my own coach was both unbelievable and completely believable. I looked at the clock. It was ten after nine. Kaz's match started at eleven.

"How'd Kaz get home?"

Manny winked.

"He here?" I said.

"He needed to relax, is what he needed to do," Manny said.

I opened the door to the guest room. Kaz lay on his stomach, on top of the sheets, wearing a shirt and no pants. The solid tan line at the middle of his thighs made it seem as if he actually were wearing a pair of shorts, but it was only his olive skin covered in a fine down. It was nothing new. I had seen him naked more than any human other than Anne.

"Kaz," I said.

He didn't move.

"Hey."

One eye opened.

"What?" He looked around.

"Manny's."

Kaz held his hand to his forehead for a moment. "Where's my pants?"

He stood unsteadily and bent to look under the bed, pointing his rear end directly towards me. Manny stepped into the doorway and said, "Hello, sailor!"

Kaz turned, his shirt falling just above his crotch, penis dangling below the hem.

"That shit was hilarious last night," Manny said.

"Where's my pants?"

"That's what I'm saying," Manny said.

"What was hilarious?" I said.

"I don't think those pants even exist anymore."

"What?" Kaz said.

"What was hilarious?"

Manny pointed at both of us and said, "I love you guys."

"Fuck," Kaz said. "I have to go, like right now."

"Here," I said, pulling a pair of my own jeans from my bag. "Take these."

Kaz slid them on without underwear. They stretched far beyond his feet. He held them up with one hand as he rushed into the hallway. I heard him bang open the door and sit with a thud. I knew he was putting on his shoes. Manny made us keep them in the hall because of their stench. After all those years, he didn't care about whether or not we were drugged or even made it to a match on time, but still our shoes couldn't enter the room.

"Manny," I said. I didn't even know where to start.

"You needed a night off. Both of you."

"Manny."

"You loved it."

"We do anything . . . ?"

"You went to India."

"With those women?"

"With those women? I love you, Slow."

"Did I . . . ?"

"No. You didn't. You just went to India and sort of looked around, pilgrimage style."

Kaz was gone. Manny plugged in the video camera. On screen appeared an image of me and Kaz, naked, slow dancing to Enya with the naked Indian women. Our arms reached around their waists like couples at my middle school dances. The woman whom I was dancing with let go and tapped the other on the shoulder, and they started dancing together. Kaz and I put our arms around each other and started to slow dance. Beside me, Manny covered his face with his hands and laughed. Kaz put his head on my shoulder, and we swayed together, naked, holding each other gently. Before long, the women tore us apart, and we started dancing with them again.

"Didn't that feel good?" Manny said.

I didn't answer.

"You don't have to say it, but I know," Manny said. "It felt good."

In the bathroom I found that someone had written SLOW'S PENIS in magic marker on my penis. I knew who had written it, too. It was my handwriting. I stared at the letters and wondered what I would have been doing at home. I knew. I would have been doing nothing. I looked at myself in the mirror, haggard and nervous and thrilled. Manny was right. I felt alive, dangerous. Free. I had my name written on my penis, and it did feel good.

9

OFF THE SUBWAY in Queens, I emerged from a covered bridge to a cobblestone courtyard surrounded by buildings with exposed beams set against stucco, as if they had been constructed from gingerbread and frosting. Trees hung low over narrow streets. It was like I'd entered some Tudor fiefdom, a tony fairyland in Queens. Forest Hills. An English village off the G train.

I rushed through four tree-lined blocks to the West Side Tennis Club. This was hallowed tennis ground. The U.S. Open had been held here until 1977, when Connors beat Vilas in a match played two months after I was born. Back when tennis meant wooden racquets and serve and volley, when the Open was played on grass, players rustling silently over manicured lawns just browning at the service line and net, when the crowds were hushed masses from country clubs. White balls. And the smell, I knew the smell; it was still the smell here, and at Wimbledon, at Queen's Club, Newport. It was still the smell in Chapel Hill beside my mother's lawn in late afternoons in the summer. It was the fragrance of a freshly mowed lawn.

They still had challenger tournaments at Forest Hills, lower-level professional events for journeymen warming up for the majors. Kaz and I had won our first tournament ever here, in 2000, and had won the doubles title for six years in a row. We had never lost a match here. It was a club record.

From the curb, the clubhouse was small and low-lying, another gingerbread construction of timber and plaster overgrown with ivy and saddled with courts on either side. Like a country house in the Cotswolds, a lodge for the weary of Queens. It reminded me of the club near my house as a child, where Katie and I had lifeguarded in the afternoons before fox-trotting at Junior Assembly at night.

Manny stayed behind to meet with a prospective client. I wondered if it wasn't some masked sexual escapade. Inside, a woman sat behind a massive wooden desk wearing a yellow shirt with crabs printed on it, pearls nestled into leathery cleavage. She smiled in an offhand way at me, as if she barely had time. I felt unofficial and embarrassed, naked without my tennis bag. The hallway was completely empty. The building was silent. I thought she might recognize me when I asked about Kaz, but she only said, "The Chinaman?"

I nodded.

"Court Four."

As she watched me pass, she wiped her hands on the tops of her breasts. I wondered if that was standard for women with sweaty palms. I hoped it was.

The hallway was lined with photos. Bill Tilden in 1926 playing in an actual tennis sweater. Champion women whom I could not identify floating across the lawns in large floppy hats and long layered dresses. Here was Connors with his Wilson T2000, the space-age aluminum racquet. Here was Billie Jean King still looking mostly female. Chris Everett at sixteen. And then, at the end of the hall, there were modern photos, including one of me and Kaz after our fourth win, standing with the trophy and club president at the net. Kaz looked filthy even in the photo. I towered over them both. A small brass plate read SMITH AND GLOVER, 2004 DOUBLES CHAMPIONS.

I emerged from the back of the clubhouse, where, past a dozen metal tables beneath orange and blue striped umbrellas all tilted at the same rakish angle, the velvet of sixteen grass courts stretched out, empty, without nets or lines. These were used for an ITA women's tournament later in the summer, but beyond the grass courts stood the clay courts, where balls now rose over green wind-stops hung on fences, bodies rushing past, umpires sitting atop their high chairs like lifeguards of tennis. The faint pop of balls flattening for a split second against strings drifted to my perch. The C train was passing on the elevated tracks beyond, and because of the vicinity to LaGuardia, three separate aircraft were visible, roaring low in the sky. I had heard that air traffic was the primary reason the Open had finally moved to Flushing Meadows, bending to years of noise complaints from Arias and Nastase. But I didn't believe it. Now, compared to Flushing Meadows, Forest Hills was a quaint, sound-proof paradise.

Beyond it all was the grandstand, where the finals of those Opens had been held, a majestic three-quarter circle of high, raked seating around an empty, neglected court. The crumbling structure was radiant in the morning sunlight. The stands were elegant, molded perhaps from simple concrete, but with the look of Grecian authority, sculpted eagles at precipices and an old box office window that still read TICKETS $8. Every entrance was hung with yellow caution tape.

A teenage boy was on the stadium court practicing serves. I envied him. I wanted to run him off and step onto the court, by myself, a full hopper beside me. It was a perverse tennis desire to long to serve into an empty court, but ever since my aborted attempt with the pink ball, the desire had only increased. As I watched, the teenager sent one ball jumping into the rotting wooden backdrop, rousing a group of pigeons from the shadows. They scattered against the sky with a hollow gurgle of wings. All play these days was on the outer courts, green clay surrounded by metal bleachers or a handful of folding chairs sparsely occupied by old men sitting alone, reading newspapers folded vertically. The grandstand was just a crumbling souvenir.

I sat in one of those folding chairs beside Court 4; applied sunscreen to my nose, the tops of my ears, and my bald spot; and folded my own newspaper vertically.

"Slow," someone said. It was Malik Al Arif. A dark Moroccan with a thin black goatee. Singles. Singles players didn't keep up with us. They just shared locker rooms. Malik told me about Morocco. It had been hot.

"Where you been?" he said, whispering. The chairs were set so close against the fence that anything you said could be heard on court.

"Home."

"You retire?"

"No," I said. "My wife's sick."

As he spoke, the eyes of the old men suddenly all left their newspapers in a gradual collective turn of the heads, as if watching the course of the slowest tennis ball ever. But it wasn't a tennis ball. It was a yellow dress, a freckled piece of my childhood that still made me nervous. It was Katie.

She had almost no nose to mention—it was washed away by the sunlight—only large tortoiseshell sunglasses above a sandbar of freckles stretching from cheek to cheek. Her shoulders were boyish, square and sharp. Her hair was pulled into a ponytail, and a light layer of down was backlit along her jaw. It all seemed made only for summer, somewhere, anywhere. For the first time, though, there was a world approaching that I did not know. I imagined her choking Manny. I heard her yell for him to do the monkey-style. I pictured her lips on the body of another woman.

She said, "Well well well."

"You look great," I said, and she stuck her bottom lip out, as if to say, isn't that strange. The gesture had been with her since childhood.

She pulled up one of the folding chairs beside mine—only feet away from the fence at the edge of the court—and said, "What are you doing here?"

"Came up for work."

"Looks like you're working hard."

"Don't move," I said. I was inspired. I rushed back to the clubhouse, where the outdoor bar by the patio was staffed by a young man in a tuxedo. I wondered what it was like to wear a tuxedo before noon.

"Champagne," I said.

"Bottle?"

I nodded and shrugged, sticking my own bottom lip out like Katie. The bill was $70, and when I placed Combover's card on top, the waiter said, "Dude, you got a bunch of suntan lotion," and lifted a finger to the side of his nose.

I wiped it off and became suddenly nervous, acutely aware of an elderly woman passing on the sidewalk. She looked at me, and I wondered if she was going to ask me what I was doing. She only grimaced and put a fingernail to her front tooth. Katie lit up when I approached.

"Why does champagne have to be saved for special occasions?" I said. "Not that this isn't a special occasion. In Russia they drink it like water. I trust the Russians in their regard for champagne." It was as if the Russians had taken over my tongue.

"I thought they drank vodka like water in Russia," she said.

"Vodka is the water in Russia. There's a fine line there."

"What do you know about Russia?"

She grinned slyly, knowingly. She was a teaser. A know-it-all. I held my plastic champagne flute into the air and said, "Frankenfurter."

She took a small camera out of her bag and shot. And then Anne was suddenly with us. I tasted the champagne and immediately thought it had been a bad purchase. It was sweet. Not that I didn't like sweet champagne. It was Anne. She liked only the driest of champagnes. I had memorized her palate and now reacted more strongly to her aversions than my own. No peppermint-flavored candies. No blue cheese. No endives. No licorice. Nothing too sweet. Nothing with milk chocolate. So much of what I had spent years perfecting—the acuity of another human's senses, the smallest details of the game of tennis—was now completely useless. I was watching the game, not playing. I was drinking champagne for myself.

Eventually two small Asian men emerged on court, huge tennis bags hung over their shoulders. They wore matching dark blue Adidas warm-up suits with WATTANAPANIT sewn across the back. Rama and Kama. The Indonesian twins. They were ranked in the mid-60s. They unzipped their jackets almost simultaneously. Nobody in tennis wore jackets with their names on them. It must have been Davis Cup swag. Neither could have been more than five-eight, and they wore shorts that revealed only a few inches of hairless leg above high orange socks. I knew them well. They ran down everything and threw trash at you, lobs, shots with no pace. They baffled strategy.

Kaz appeared, hanging his head as he dropped his bag at his chair. His hair was balled into a bizarre nest on the side, and he wore a shirt that had an autograph on it. It was clearly something he had just found in the locker room. Usually, if he was winning, he'd wear the same shirt every day. The same *socks*. He spent huge amounts of energy getting his winning clothes to the laundry in assorted spots across the globe. When he bought new shoes, he had to immediately scuff the top of the right toe so that the mark was visible. That was the toe that he would drag after his serve. He had to have it scuffed before he ever served with it, though. And the other foot, it could never be scuffed. It had to be perfect. Sometimes he would buy new shoes just for a clean left shoe. We got most of our shoes for free from Adidas, but when our rep heard about this tic she stopped servicing Kaz.

He draped a towel over his head.

"What's wrong with him?" Katie said.

"Manny drugged us."

"Gobstopper?"

"Yes. Does he do this?"

"It's one of his things."

Gentleman John crossed the court towards us and said, "What'd you do to him?"

"It was Manny."

John turned to the towel and said, "You went out with *Manny*?"

Kaz finally emerged and took a notepad out of his bag.

"Here we go," Katie said.

He carefully paced the length between the chair and the net post, then wrote a figure down. He counted the bananas from his bag, then noted it. He looked at the clock and wrote down the time, then closed the book and began to trade forehands with one of the Wattanapanits before stopping to write more. Throughout it all, he made sure to not step on any lines.

The umpire called time. Kaz's serve was never his strong suit, but he spun his first out wide, cutting away from one of the Wattanapanits, who swung and touched nothing. I heard the whiff through his strings. The next serve went into the other one's body, which he blocked back, floating high into the air. Kaz approached the net calmly and slammed an overhead, the ball bouncing so high that it landed outside the fence. He was careless and cavalier, as if these points were an intrusion in his otherwise busy day. He won his game at love, then sent his first return of serve down the line with a forehand passing shot, pointing towards the spot.

Katie was stoic, silent behind her sunglasses.

"You getting this?" I said.

"Yeah, I'm getting this."

"Well, come on."

She shrugged.

"Something wrong?"

She stuck out her bottom lip.

"What?"

"Nothing."

She watched Kaz hit a leaping overhead backhand, spinning as he landed, her beautiful head moving to watch the ball cut between the twins at the net. It settled into the hands of a young ball girl, who bent like a robot to settle the ball.

"I'll tell you later."

She watched a miss-hit service return fly off a Wattanapanit frame and float high into the sun. She kept her eyes pointed towards the sky for a second longer than needed, her face falling only after the ball had already landed. I wondered if it was the residue of adolescence that biased me, that had me still convinced that she was the pinnacle of beauty. I loved Anne, but her greatest fault was that she was not Katie. She could never do anything about it.

After one long rally, more than a dozen strokes, one of the Wattanapanits finally hit a short ball, and Kaz drilled it down the line. He pumped his fist, and I yelled, "Come on!"

Katie looked at me blankly. There was a scar on her lip that I had forgotten, a bite from a dog in elementary school. It seemed to make her even more perfect.

I said, "Don't feel sorry for me because I'm not playing."

"It's not that," she said and poured more champagne. "Just ignore me. I'm in a weird mood."

A few times throughout the rest of the match she cheered, but I could tell she didn't mean it. I kept it up, though, yelling at the top of my lungs. Mostly I didn't mean it either. I just didn't want anyone to know how jealous I was.

10

YOUNG MEN IN crumpled athletic gear ate pasta off chipped event china beside silent old women in pearls and their patrician husbands in boat shoes talking incessantly about their own tennis games. Paunches circled each other in packs before breaking off into individual paunch satellites to give a player a pat on the back. It was close to ninety degrees even when the sun was down, and I was sweating on the porch outside the dining room, drunk. Kaz was eating so much pesto penne that I could only think of it scientifically.

"Slow was about to have a heart attack," Katie said.

"It's harder to watch," Kaz said.

"I mean cheering for you."

I ordered more champagne, but the waiter, a young man with an Eastern European accent, told me only beer was free. I gave him Combover's Visa. I had used it so many times already that I was starting to think of it as my own.

"You a player?" he said.

"Yeah."

"I'll see what I can work out. What's your name?"

"You don't have to work anything out."

"No, really. Sometimes it's no problem."

Katie looked at her feet.

"I'm not playing this week," I said. "Just put it on the card."

After he returned with the bottle, a young man with a thick blond beard and thin, greasy dreadlocks approached from across the patio. I'd grown up playing him, through juniors and up. His name was Ben Gables. But no one called him by his real name. They just called him Brah.

"Real pain for my sham friends," Brah said. "Champagne for my real friends."

Kaz nodded, his mouth full.

"Kazuhiro, you my hero."

Katie took the champagne bottle from the table and walked with it towards the edge of the patio. She stepped past the edge of the light and into the dark grass of the empty courts. I waved to Brah and followed. We padded across those netless courts like we were in a carpeted museum after hours. It felt soft and illicit, and we didn't stop until the grandstand loomed before us. I imagined the matches captured in those photos that lined the clubhouse walls. It was hard for me to picture the actual events in color. This had been the epicenter of American tennis, and now it was the dark space that halted Katie and me in our flight from Brah. Inside those stands were the old locker rooms, where Arthur Ashe and Clark Graebner actually took showers between sets in the '60s, where the national tennis mystique was cultivated. I had once convinced a groundsman to let me in. Those rooms no longer had electricity. The locker rooms we used were now in the clubhouse, the very same ones used by the members playing slow-motion doubles on Sunday afternoons with knee braces. Kaz and I owned Forest Hills, but it was like getting the keys to Atlantis. The magic was gone. Katie caught my eye as she turned away. She knew where she was going. At the end of the path dim lights glimmered on the undulating surface of the pool.

On the Fourth of July before I started sixth grade, Reginald Edwards, the lifeguard at the Chapel Hill Country Club, held a jar of pennies beside the pool and swept his arm out before him, sending the coins through the air in a widening copper arc. Sunlight glittered off the newest ones before they spattered into the deep end. Katie and I dove after them with the rest of the kids. As our competitors failed under the pressure of twelve feet of water and rose, we held out, snatching those glimmering coins off the bottom with our wrinkled fingertips. We were masters of the pool. We spent every possible day there. Katie tanned from morning to dusk while I cooled off between sets played on courts only yards away. After the pennies, Reginald dumped a bucket of goldfish into the pool. Katie and I captured the most quivering creatures, our fingertips grazing each other as we reached towards the same elusive fish. They wriggled through the water like pennies come alive. When Reginald tossed the greased watermelon into the deep end, we stayed on our chaises. This task was only for adults. But when father after father emerged empty-handed, laughing and blowing their noses, it became clear that the melon was not coming up. I moved. Reginald's voice disappeared in midshout as my head passed into that blue other world. The green oval was dark and heavy below. I pushed it across the tiled pool bottom until it reached the shallow end, where I could lift it into the sunlight. Before I did, though, I opened my eyes underwater and looked up. The shifting form of Katie stood poolside. I said, "I love you," and a mass of bubbles came out of my mouth and rose to the surface, exploding silently into the air above.

Katie stood poolside again. This time she was in the dark, and I was behind her. I could barely see her as she lifted her dress. The fabric wadded up around her neck, revealing a headless torso in underwear. I looked around, terrified someone else might see. She struggled to release her arms. Finally her head popped out. She dropped the dress and dove. There was a tiny splash, a few droplets of water splattered onto my face, and for one moment I was the only one above ground. Then she surfaced, whipped her hair back, and said, "Come on."

One

This was my coach's wife.

Two

And I was a married man.

Three

Four

Five

"Slow."

I took off my clothes in such a rush that I fell while pulling off my pants. Katie laughed, and when I finally got up and dove, her smile was so wide that, as I flew through the air, I saw her molars, small hidden pearlescent spots gleaming dimly in the back of her mouth.

The water hit me like an ice bath. I could barely catch my breath, inhaling sharply as I emerged. I drifted towards Katie, and when I was close enough that I could see her eyes reflecting the light from the clubhouse, I said, "I knew you were going to get in."

"Don't act like you know everything about me," she said and put a hand on top of my head. She pushed down, and I let myself plummet, the blue darkening around me like a theater before a play. But the actors in this drama were Katie's legs, kicking dark and mechanical before me. I watched them with as much wonder as anything on a real stage. When I surfaced, Jimmy Buffett was drifting thinly over the grass courts, through the grandstand, and over the water.

"I used to love this song," Katie said.

"I know," I said.

"Don't act like you know everything about me," she said again, softly, an afterthought. We floated in silence on our backs, listening to Jimmy Buffett and looking up at the stars, interspersed with blinking airplanes like bits of the firmament come to life.

After a while, I said, "You gonna tell me what you've been thinking about?"

She said nothing. I paddled with only one hand and spun myself in a slow circle.

"I'm sorry about you and Manny."

"He's an asshole."

"He told me that he was emailing all those people and stuff."

An airplane flew low in the sky above, its roar pressing down, lights blinking some urgent message. Katie swam to the small ladder on the side of the pool and hung on to the chrome rail. I grabbed the other side. She said, "You keeping up with Anne's project?"

I nodded. "I got the nurse to shoot it while I was gone."

"I've seen stuff like that do really well."

"What does that mean?"

She held her hand into the air like it was an explanation. "If you keep doing it she could really have something when she wakes up."

"Can I tell you something?"

"Whew," she said. "That line always makes me nervous."

I swung closer to her and caught her foot underwater. I placed it flush against my stomach and held it there, like a power source, some mystical hormone machine pumping extra blood into my veins. It was stupid and sexy. When she wiggled her toes it was like a bite on a long still line. Something rushed through me that hadn't visited my system in ages. I put my other hand on her prickly calf, and a man yelled, "Cannonball!"

I turned towards the sound and saw backlit dreadlocks glowing lightly around their fuzzy edges. I let go of Katie's foot as an explosion of water burst over us. Brah appeared at the surface, grinning and laughing.

"Couldn't find you guys," he said.

"Who are you?" Katie said.

"Brah."

"Brah, could you leave us alone?" she said.

"Whoa," he said, laughing. "You guys getting it on?"

"Yeah. We're getting it on," Katie said.

He swam to the ladder and turned, water pouring in a small stream from each dreadlock.

"Aren't you married?" he said.

"Yeah. I'm married," I said.

"Go," Katie said. "Jesus."

He put his hands in front of his face, as if he were warding off a wild animal, then backed away, into the darkness. We watched his silhouette grow smaller as he passed over the grass and disappeared.

"I hate that guy," I said.

"He's not the one you should hate," Katie said.

"What do you mean?"

"Can I tell you something?"

That line did inspire terror. I started to laugh, but there was no humor on her face. She was serious. My chuckle faded to Jimmy Buffett, and then she told me who I should hate.

I exhaled and sank, the blue depth darkening like the show had just begun again after a long intermission.

11

AN OFF-BALANCE CEILING fan wobbled around in the humidity. Manny sprawled across the tiny couch, spider limbs reaching halfway across the room. Without a shirt, his few chest hairs struggled off his protruding ribs and held themselves into the heat like sparse, wilting weeds.

"You remember how the vegetables in the Harris Teeter get sprayed with that automated mist?" he said. "Hey, I'm talking to you!"

I walked past him and into the bathroom, where I spit long strings of saliva into the bowl, waiting for vomit.

By the time I emerged, Manny had disappeared. I took his place on the couch, the cushions still warm from his massive frame. The dog jumped out the back window. I put my hands on my face and sighed. I was in the same position twenty minutes later, when Manny returned with a brown paper bag in each hand and a bundle of plastic tubing under an arm. He wore a sweat-soaked white tank top and one long strand of greasy hair drooped from his pompadour over an eye. His giant lips were stretched into a huge smile.

"Slow," he said. "We're going to be like those vegetables."

"OK."

"You alright?"

I shrugged.

"Don't you want to know where I've been?"

I shrugged.

"Continental Carbonic." He nodded his head. "Dry ice, my friend. Slow! What's wrong with you?"

I watched like a zombie as he filled three cooking pots, his only cooking pots, with water, then placed them in the corners of the living room. He shook small white pellets out of the bags and, as they dropped, hissing, into the water, steam poured over the edges. The currents from the ceiling fan moved the mist in an undulating swirl across the hardwood floor, slowly parting around my ankles like a shifting carpet of cloud. Manny hung the tubes from hooks left in the ceiling for the ghosts of Katie's hanging plants. He dropped the ends into the pots of dry ice. Steam then tumbled onto our heads, falling over our shoulders and finally meeting the undulating mass still hovering at the floor.

"I'm a vegetable," Manny said. "Slow! What the fuck's your problem? This is magic!"

I looked up at the wobbling fan and watched the indoor clouds land cold on my eyes, imaging what would happen if they froze and shattered, falling in pieces out of my face. My cell phone rang, and Manny said, "Yours, freak."

I closed my eyes, took a deep breath, then picked up my phone. It was Kaz.

"Where'd you go?" he said.

The phone shook in my hand. I said, "Brah." It was enough explanation.

"Manny have any more gobstopper?"

I looked at Manny, stretched out on the mini couch in his underwear, the dog draped across his lap.

"It's gobstopper central," I said.

Manny's intercom had a small video screen on which you could see the person at the door. When Kaz buzzed, I watched the grainy image of him, shifting from foot to foot. His hair was still in that greasy ponytail. I thought of the last grainy image of him I'd seen, dancing naked in my arms. I pushed ENTER.

"This safe?" Kaz said, stepping into the fog.

"Feel how it's cooling things off?" Manny said.

"I gotta get some more of that medicine."

"But seriously. Shit is cold, right?"

"No."

"No gobstopper for you."

"I played out of my mind today," he said. "I got to do it again."

"I'll get it for you," I said.

"Slow," Manny said. But I knew where it was. In the refrigerator I'd seen a baby-food container with a skull and crossbones drawn on it. I recognized Manny's handiwork. I took the container out and opened it. The stuff smelled like nothing. I filled a shot glass halfway.

"That'll kill him," Manny said, then took the glass from me. Over the sink he carefully poured it back into the skull jar without losing a drop. "Seriously." He poured one small trickle into the cap of the jar. "Here."

Kaz opened his mouth, and Manny poured in the capful.

"You want more?" I said.

Kaz nodded.

"I'm serious," Manny said. "Any more will kill him."

"I'm not going to kill him," I said and opened the fridge.

"Hey!" Manny said and stood.

I took out the jar, unscrewed the lid, and refilled it.

Manny reached his wiry arm through the fog and smacked the cap out of my hand, sending gobstopper splattering through the indoor clouds.

"I don't know what is wrong with you," Manny said. "But you need to chill out. Right now."

I sat on the miniature couch and stared at Manny's Ouija board, propped against the wall beside a large pile of Westerns on VHS.

"Can you only talk to dead people through a Ouija board?" I said.

"You don't have to be dead to have a spirit," Manny said, still annoyed.

"Then let's do it."

"Really?"

"Yeah."

He was suddenly at ease, the gobstopper forgotten.

"Alright," he said, giddy. "This shit is crazy. Seriously. You're going to love it."

He retrieved the board from behind the videos and spread it across the little coffee table. It covered the whole surface. It was the same Parker Brothers model that I'd had as a middle schooler, with the alphabet printed in gothic lettering above a YES and NO under a moon and sun.

"What are you doing?" Kaz said from the kitchen, where he was looking in cabinets.

"We're going to talk to the spirit world," Manny said.

"We're going to talk to Anne," I said.

Manny stopped in the middle of wiping something off the board and looked up.

"Whoa. OK. Now you guys have to keep an open mind," he said. "I've been getting into this. I've been breaking through some barriers."

I sat cross-legged on the floor.

"I don't know," Kaz said.

"Sit down," Manny said.

We placed our fingertips on the plastic viewer.

"Lightly," Manny said. "Easy."

Kaz looked from Manny to me nervously, licking his gums.

"Anne," Manny said. "It's Manny and Kaz and Slow. Talk to us, girl."

I waited, maybe more than a minute. The plastic thing sat motionless beneath our fingers. When the apprehension began to fade and Manny and Kaz showed the first signs of surrender—yawning and looking around—that was when I started to push.

Their faces slackened in amazement.

I stopped the viewer on the letter H, then moved.

I

"Holy shit," Kaz whispered.

G

U

Y

S

"Holy *shit!*"

"Shhh," Manny said.

"You pushing it?" Kaz said.

"No."

"Seriously."

"Shhh. No."

The fog was too perfect. It rolled around our fingers, under the plastic viewer, and over the table edge. I let the silence play out. Then I pushed again.

T

E

L

L

H

I

M

"Tell who?" Manny said.

On this stage Kaz became the lead actor, his face falling into a comic visage of terror.

"Tell what?" Manny said. "Who tell what?"

I didn't move it for quite a while this time, and unbelievably, the viewer actually moved on account of itself, that magical force of fingers and nervous energy that had blown middle school minds for decades. I let it drift around for a moment and wondered if Anne might actually try to take this odd mouthpiece over before I took charge again and spelled:

K

A

Z

"I swear to God, if you guys are pushing this," Kaz whispered.

"We're not pushing it," Manny said.

"This is Anne," I said.

"I don't have anything to tell you," Kaz said. "She must mean you tell me something." But as he spoke, I began to move it again.

N

O

Y

O

U

K

A

Z

T

E

L

L

S

L

O

W

Kaz looked at me. He blinked rapidly, his pupils black holes beneath the fluttering eyelids.

A

B

O

U

T

All three of us leaned in, the last letters spelling, very slowly

U

S

Kaz took his fingers off the board and lay back, onto the floor.

"What the fuck?" Manny said.

"Why'd you give me that stuff?" he said.

"Focus, man," Manny said. "Anne just asked you to do something."

"Oh my God."

"Hey," I said. "Sit up."

Kaz sat up.

"There something you need to tell me?"

Kaz looked at the board, the viewer still atop the S. He picked up the board and inspected it closely, flipped it over, then set it back down.

"I'm really fucked-up right now."

"That's OK," Manny said. "Just go with it."

"What was she talking about?" I said.

Kaz said nothing.

"Tell him," Manny said.

"What was it?"

"Say it," Manny said.

Kaz shook his head.

"What? Say it," I said.

"Say it!" Manny said.

But Kaz wouldn't say it. Finally, after a moment of silence, he looked up. Any doubt disappeared with the look on his face.

"We . . ." He looked back and forth between the two of us. "Did I already tell you?"

A small indoor cloud blew in front of him. "We did it."

I had never shed a tear before either of them, but now it wouldn't stop. I put my hands on my face, tears running through my fingers and down my arms.

"Oh my God," Kaz said. "I can't think about any of this." He stood. "I'm sorry, man. I . . ." His eyes were crazy. He began to walk away, one arm against the wall for support.

I breathed deeply, trying to gain control, and saw Manny looking at me, unsurprised and fascinated, as if he knew exactly what was happening.

"You knew?" I said.

He stuck out his huge bottom lip and shrugged.

"And you didn't tell me?"

"The other person never needs to know."

"That she was sleeping with him?"

He held his hand towards me as if I were on display. "Not really."

I looked at my best friends, my business partners, my coach and my doubles partner in the mist before me. These were the people I had always been able to speak to. But there was nothing my lips could conjure. I felt like the dry ice had frozen me.

One

Kaz's hand slid across the old rough stucco as he staggered slow and jagged into the hall.

Two

Manny looked right at me, his eyebrows high on his forehead in apprehension. He was ready for action.

Three

Four

Manny looked at Kaz and then back at me.

Five

Six

"Kaz," I said. And he stopped, pausing under one of the tubes. Fog rushed onto his head like water from a spigot.

Seven

Some animal reaction was required here, something I was too analytic to produce. Manny was the only person I could imagine proceeding with appropriate passion.

Seven

Manny nodded at me, as if to say, you're all right, get to it. But I didn't know what to get to. So I tried to imagine I was him. I pouted my lips. I sneered. I searched myself for brute impulse.

Eight

On the mantel over Manny's shoulder stood a VHS copy of *High Noon*, an illustrated Gary Cooper on the cover with one gun at his shoulder—smoke trailing from the barrel—and another at his hip, pointed right at me.

Nine

For a moment it all seemed clear. I said, "I want to duel."

"Huh?" Kaz said. He held out his hands, like he was warding off an imminent attack.

"Oh *yeah*," Manny whispered.

Kaz waved his hand as if the fog were impeding his progress. "You mean fight?"

"I mean duel," I said. But I didn't know what I meant. I just wanted to let myself talk, allow whatever nonsense was inside of me to come out. Like Manny would, to be fearless and trusting of instinct. Kaz continued to move the fog with his palms, then took two wavering steps into the guest room. I watched the door for a moment, expecting him to reemerge, but he didn't. He was gone, only feet away. But I wasn't done. I was high on the act of channeling Manny. I stood and walked to the door. I looked in. He lay on his stomach on the mattress, eyes closed.

"He'll be fine," Manny said.

One leg dangled off the side. It was bad for his back, and if he didn't move at some point he was going to have a hard time serving, and when Kaz had a hard time serving nothing else in his game worked. I tried to put it out of my mind. I shouldn't care. I turned to Manny and said, "Why didn't you tell me?"

"Slow. This is *exactly* how this should be handled."

"OK, fine. But why didn't you *tell* me?"

"I'll set it up. We'll do it on court. It'll be a tennis duel."

"Forget about the duel," I said. I already regretted the ridiculous challenge. "Hey!"

"'Cause you didn't need to know! But this was different, man. Anne was just here with us. She *wanted* you to know." Manny paced the room, thrilled with the confusion of life.

"Anne wasn't here."

"Is this going to be sweet—what?"

"Anne wasn't here."

"You have to open your mind."

"I was pushing it."

For a moment he untangled what I had done, then said, "Slow. Damn! After my own heart, brother. How'd you know?"

"Katie told me."

He shook his head and said, "Slow. You're doing the right thing."

"Jesus! Forget about the duel."

"No sir. Wait. Wait! Where you going?"

"I don't know."

But I knew. I walked out of the apartment and into the warm night. I couldn't listen to him draw up any more plans to duel. I was increasingly mortified. I told myself Kaz wouldn't remember a word of what had been said. I took three steps to the sidewalk in slow, measured steps. The street was awash with young people. I dried my eyes, and two young women watched me as they passed. It felt like the first time I'd ever been noticed on a New York City sidewalk. Let them look. Who were they? The only person I wanted to see was in a new apartment four blocks away.

12

KATIE'S BRASS BUZZER glimmered within a frame of caked white polish, years of it rubbed into each crack of the marble jamb. I pressed the pearl beside her name. She answered, relaxed and happy. Immune to the tiny explosions of my erratic life.

"It's Slow," I said, and the door began to buzz.

On the third floor, I exited the elevator to a lobby with one door ajar. I gently swung it open. Here, the rooms had furniture. The walls were hung with paintings above paintings surrounded by framed photos. Above me the second floor reached out in a small interior balcony.

"Up here," Katie called.

I ascended a curving flight of stairs. On the wall beside me hung an old photo of two naked boys boxing in a field, surrounded by a ring of other naked boys sitting in a circle around them, laughing. Another showed steel girders, cropped close, dark and angular and heavy. I couldn't imagine decorating a space like this, finding these objects and hanging them, and it then occurred to me that people like Katie, they didn't do these things themselves. They had people do it for them. She could call one of the galleries she worked with and within an hour have a van filled with men in blue jumpsuits and white gloves. It was unbelievable to me that she had ever even lived in Manny's apartment. This space was so clearly hers.

On the landing, one wall was lined with African masks above a small fireplace with an actual fire burning inside. It gave off no heat.

Beside it Katie sat erect on a love seat, joined on the cushion by Paige. Both were dressed in white. Lit by the flickering flames, they looked like they were preparing for some religious rite. Katie wore a simple cotton dress, but Paige's white blouse had enough starch in it that it could stand up on its own. Her lipstick was so red that it was the first time I had ever thought of makeup as scandalous. Opera played softly from unseen speakers.

"Slow," Katie said. "This is Paige."

"It is very nice to meet you," Paige said, her robot accent even more rigid than it had been before.

I shook her hand and tried to not make eye contact. The electricity of secret filled the room. It seemed impossible that Katie couldn't feel it.

"What are you doing?" Katie said.

"Kaz came over to Manny's," I said. And then, before I said another word, the tears welled up. I put my face in my hands. Katie patted the space between herself and Paige. I fell into it, touching more female thigh than I had in nine months.

"You told him you knew?" Katie said.

I nodded.

"What'd he say?"

"I challenged him to a duel."

"A duel?"

"A tennis duel," I said and started to cry outright.

No one spoke. I guess they were at a loss. Most people had been at a loss with me since the accident. In a way, I savored it. It gave me a type of power over the social moment. I let my drying eyes fall to the photo album in Katie's lap and found myself looking back from her sixth-grade birthday party. That was the year that, after watching boys carve snakes into their shoulders in the movie *Stand by Me*, I had scratched KATIE into my own shoulder with a pocket knife. I never showed it to Katie, but rather cultivated the fantasy that she would discover it one day by chance, maybe find me sleeping or see me from across a classroom and glimpse that scabbed token of obsession peeking out under my shirtsleeve. Within days of the act the name grew swollen and too rich with pus to hold it all. In my embarrassment, I did not tell my parents until my whole arm became so sore that I couldn't play tennis. When they saw what I had done, neither my parents nor my doctor asked for an explanation. They just treated Katie's name with antibiotics, ignoring the boyish lust behind it. That was the same year Katie showed me the illustrated instructions that came in a box of tampons and asked me if I had ever had sex. As if there were a chance I had. A month later, she asked me if I would show her a boner. We were on the phone, though, so I couldn't show her anything, but I told her I would sometime, and weeks later, at that birthday party—the one in the photo I was looking at now—we danced to Salt-N-Pepa on a boom box in her garage, and she whispered, "Boner. Boner." I said, "There it is." It was pressed against her pelvis. And that was it. We just kept on dancing, as if I were not shaking, blood vessels bursting, envisioning the future of the memory even then, knowing it was momentous, knowing that, at least for me, it would haunt.

Katie said, "You really said you wanted to duel?"

I nodded and laughed.

"That's badass."

Of course she thought so. It was Manny's logic, not my own.

I flipped through more of the album. At age three or four, Katie straddled a small motorcycle in the lap of a teenage uncle. In fifth grade she tanned poolside with her headgear on. She still looked beautiful with that plastic halo holding shining hooks in her mouth. As a toddler, she held an unlit cigarette to her lips while her family laughed. I stood on a tennis court at the club, so tall and thin it reminded me of my growing pains. And then she flipped a page to a Polaroid of an azalea in bloom. It was like Anne had entered the room.

"Why did you guys get this out?" I said.

"Paige wanted to see me as a girl."

"How do you know each other?"

"Through Manny," Katie said. Paige sat silent beside her, her eyes cast down at the photos.

"Do you live here in New York City?" Paige said.

"No," I said. "I live in North Carolina. Where do you live?"

"Fifty-second Street."

"That's how you know Manny?"

She nodded.

I said, "I've been staying over there."

"Stay here tonight," Katie said.

"I am staying too," Paige said. "It is a slumber party."

As the girls got ready for bed, I stayed on the love seat looking at photos. Everything seemed to have just happened, no matter what I saw. Roller-skating at age nine was just yesterday. My hair—it had been there just days ago. While I stretched a thin blanket across the couch, Paige emerged from Anne's bedroom in a red Japanese robe and whispered, "Thank you."

"But what's the secret?"

"You are so cute," she said and hugged me, her body soft under my arms. It reminded me of the shift Anne's skin had made in the last few months of her pregnancy as her thin torso filled out, her limbs becoming soft where they once were hard, all of her flesh infused with a thin layer of give. When Paige let go, she went back into Katie's room and waved as the door swung shut.

I knew what Manny had told me. Katie had kissed those lips. They weren't only having a slumber party beyond those doors. For one moment I thrilled myself by considering joining them in the bedroom, but that thrill soon turned to fear. I surprised myself by falling asleep almost immediately. I guess I had used up everything left. The night was filled with nightmares and dreams of strange sexual scenarios. Everything was mixed up. Everyone seemed to love everyone and hate everyone at the same time, and I felt terrified and left out.

13

IN THE MORNING the three of us walked to Manny's apartment to steal the Fiat. Katie and Paige found the car while I snuck inside for my bag. Kaz was asleep on the bed. Again he wore no pants. Two rats scurried from out of a potato chip bag in the corner and rushed under the bed. On their way one ran over the top of my foot. I tried not to jump. I didn't want to wake Kaz. I wanted to look at him.

He had almost no body hair, just one dark mound of thick wire above his uncircumcised penis. I stood there at the foot of the bed and imagined my wife holding that body, lying atop it. Kissing it.

One of Manny's Sharpies was on the bedside table, and I took the lid off, picked up Kaz's immaculate left shoe, and drew an X on it. Then I opened his backpack and found a small, hard-backed black sketchpad. It was his journal. He always used the same kind and had changed volumes only a handful of times because of the brevity of his entries. I opened it to a page that said I ORANGE GATORADE, I GRAPE GATORADE, I GRAPE GATORADE, 2 BOTTLES WATER ON COURT (CRYSTAL SPRING). 82 DEGREES. 2 BANANAS AT SET BREAK. I put it in the pocket of my jacket, then picked up the potato chip bag and silently sprinkled the contents around him on the bed, letting them fall where a rat might most easily find them.

Outside, the girls were already in the Fiat. The car was running. I put my bag in the trunk and sat on top of it, my legs dangling into the interior space behind the two passenger seats. Katie hit the gas, and I held tightly to her headrest and yelled into the wind, "I'm not riding like this the whole way up there."

Paige said, "I have devised a way for all three of us to ride."

In the street in front of Katie's apartment I loaded their bags into the trunk, from which I first had to remove a strange collection of brightly painted pottery wrapped in newspaper. Paige then emerged from inside carrying the long red cushion from the love seat. She laid it across the passenger seat and emergency brake. There was just enough clearance for the gearshift.

"Now this coupe seats three," she said.

"Coupe?"

"Car."

"But that blocks the seat belt."

Paige ignored me and climbed into the middle, positioning her legs on either side of the gear hub, the shifter standing rigid between her legs.

"I'm not going to ride without my seat belt," I said.

"You just rode without even sitting in a seat."

"I didn't like it."

"You can reach the seat belt on that side," Paige said, pointing to the steering wheel.

I had not driven since the accident. I had resigned myself to walking, biking, taking the Chapel Hill bus system to the grocery store, relying on friends to take me to dinner, calling a cab for a dentist appointment. Now Katie was already arranging herself in the passenger seat, adjusting her purse at her feet. I looked around, as if someone might help. There was no one on the block except for an old lady walking three pugs. So I got in the driver's seat, buckled up, put my hand on that rod protruding from Paige's crotch, and shifted into first.

It was a Wednesday morning, late, so the traffic was light, and we rolled up the West Side Highway under the speed limit, the boats wobbling against a glimmering Hudson in the Boat Basin to our left.

We were going to Katie's mountain house. Paige took charge of the radio and somehow found opera again.

There was no third gear, which meant I had to muscle that shifter out of and back into Paige's crotch in one violent motion to shift from second to fourth.

"I must say I admire your restraint in regard to the speed limit," Paige said as I shifted out of her crotch and into fifth coming over the George Washington Bridge.

We passed a tourist bus filled with Japanese families who all crowded the windows to take our picture. I guess to them a young man and two beautiful women in a green Fiat convertible with bull-horns was probably like us seeing a rickshaw filled with geishas in Tokyo. Paige waved.

"Do you not like driving?" she said.

Katie had shown Paige photos of me in my awkward years, and probably earlier, but had apparently made no mention of my wife. The thought that she was guarding that complicated knowledge made me feel safe as we sped through the salty air over the Hudson while a woman on the radio sustained a high vibrato note, leaving the waving Japanese to their daydreams of our American road trip. I shrugged, as if to say, *Driving, it's not all bad.* My thoughts drifted away from Anne and Kaz, and as I passed over that water, I felt like I was just floating.

We rolled upstate along a river with bodies floating by on large rubber inner tubes in the opposite direction; past a railroad with a sightseeing train traveling at a snail's pace along the river; between steep canyons and crashing white water, the air cooling precipitously and opera still on; and finally, two hours later, up a driveway, cut into the side of a mountain, that wound back and forth for more than a mile until we came to a gravel clearing at a weathered green clapboard house with cedar shingles and a broken-down BMW in the driveway with TOW brushed in soap across the windshield.

Three Adirondack chairs and a hammock were worn but looked like they would last decades more, bought with some impossible Katie knowledge. Standing in the high grass was a large bull sculpted from dark, weather-stained bronze. A tarnished brass candelabra half full of melted burgundy candle stubs stood on the porch, miniature mountains of wax reaching up towards their sources from the floorboards. Inside the sun-filled living room, an old Sunday *Times* was scattered across wide wooden floorboards before a scuffed leather couch. For the first time the truth hit me that Katie had left the geography of our childhood behind. She now had roots in this cold state. The streets of her dog-walking from the pool were occupied by only me now, walking the soft tar alone with a single pink tennis ball.

Immediately Paige opened the fridge and started making a list. Katie disappeared into a bedroom. I sat on a high metal shop stool beside a worn chopping block, and my cell phone began to ring. I took it out of my pocket and looked at the display.

"It's Manny," I said.

"So?"

"Mind if I answer?"

Before Paige could respond, Katie entered the room, and I slid the phone back into my pocket.

"What is the co-op number again?" Paige said.

Katie rattled off a string of digits.

"Company card," I said, handing her Combover's Visa. "It's for expenses."

She shrugged and put the card into her jeans.

My room had a doorway that was too short for my head and a view of the backyard, which was expansive and ended at the edge of a pond, where a narrow dock stretched twenty feet into the water. The sun was low over the line of trees at the far edge of the lake, and countless shattered pieces of it undulated in a brilliant display across the surface. The bed was narrow and hard, and there was one simple chest of drawers that looked like it had been in this very room since the day the house was built. I opened the top drawer. Inside were four framed photos of Manny and Katie, some shriveled marijuana in a plastic bag, and a small metal pipe. Katie said, "Looking for drugs?"

She stood in the doorway. She had changed into a white dress and a straw hat that I recognized as once having been Manny's.

"Want to do some?"

"Sure," I said.

"I'm gonna stroll before the sun goes down," she said, ignoring me. If she had said OK, I would have smoked that marijuana. In this place I felt like I could become someone else. I felt the compulsion to.

"I would prefer an escort," she said.

Two parallel gravel strips with a median of weeds led into the trees along the water. The sun was not yet down, and a few green leaves blew off the oak trees as we walked, falling in slow spirals, lit by the horizontal beams of sunlight. A gigantic tree lay in the pond, fallen from its perch on the bank, leaving its roots grasping for air above an earthen crater. I stepped into the hole where those roots had once held earth and looked up. A great heron flew overhead, low, squawking a guttural cry through its massive folded neck, and we both watched it pass, bending our heads skyward. I had spent so many hundreds of hours under varying skies, but it was always on a cleared surface, a coated space, a concrete rectangle or a clay court or a small patch of mowed and manicured grass. I hadn't walked through nature in what felt like decades.

"You look like a little boy," Katie said.

"I feel like one."

Our parallel gravel strips led us to the far edge of the pond, from where we could see a single ramshackle house on the opposite bank.

"I wish I could live in that house year-round," Katie said.

"Whose is it?"

She looked at me like I was crazy. "That's my house."

I couldn't believe it was the very house I had just been in. It was too small, too run-down. From inside it had seemed so spacious. Katie had asserted the same architectural magic upon it as she had on Manny's apartment.

"Think that thing works?" she said.

"What thing?"

"That."

She pointed towards a dark space under the low branch of a live oak tree. I looked more closely. In the shadow rested a green paddle-boat with a muddy white wheel.

"It yours?"

She shrugged and stuck out her bottom lip. "It's always been there."

"Let's."

"Really?"

"They used to call me Slow, but now they call me Fast," I said.

"Now they call you a huge dork," she said. I kicked the plastic side of the paddleboat, and it resonated deep and plastic. "Sounds seaworthy to me."

It floated, sure enough, and we pedalled ourselves into the middle of the pond. The sun cast its final rays on the tops of the trees on the bank from where we had departed. The tips of the oaks glowed orange, the leaves like fading embers. It was the moment I had been waiting for for almost twenty years. I was alone on a pond with a single Katie. She was looking down, and I reached for her hand. She squeezed firmly, looked up, the sky glowing a deep purple behind her, and said, "We're sinking."

I looked at my feet. Water was rapidly filling the bottom of the boat, already inches high. Katie laughed. I took the hat off her head and began bailing water with it, the water pouring back into the boat through the hundreds of small holes in the weave. The craft was sinking precipitously. We abandoned ship, swimming away as it tilted onto its side like a mammoth steamer sinking in the distance on an old newsreel.

At its widest point, the pond stretched probably three hundred yards from shore to shore. We had swum lengths like this for fun dozens of times, had had breath-holding contests that lasted minutes. Katie swam well ahead of me towards the house, her dress trailing in a rippling white wake. Between surfacing for air, bobbing in and out of that murky water, she pulled up, smiled, and said, "Hey, you want to—" and I knew she was going to say *race*, but she bobbed low, and for a brief moment the surface of the pond rose higher than her bottom lip, and she inhaled. Her eyes widened playfully, as if she had forgotten we were still a hundred yards from the bank. She tried to cough, but nothing came out.

A sense of inevitability seemed to swoop low over the pond. This was simply what happened now: If you were female, and spoke with me, or left the house with me, or walked around a pond with me, or—let alone—if I happened to be in love with you, then you were going to suffer a terrible trauma, and I was going to see it, and I wasn't going to be able to stop it, and it was going to be my fault.

By the time I reached her, her eyes were wild, wide and shifting, surprised that this could happen, of all people, to her. She strained against her saturated lungs. I put my arms around her and squeezed. All that happened was I tipped her face directly into the water. I wrapped my arm around her chest, my left hand deep in her armpit, and swam. As I kicked towards land she went limp.

I wondered if, when I called the police, they were going to bring up my records and see that my wife had almost died in my arms within the same year and think it was too much of a coincidence. I wondered if they would find that Dart at Al's Garage and finally inspect the brake pedal that they had never even looked at, if they would charge me with murder, or attempted murder, because in truth I felt they should.

Near the bank my feet settled into an invisible slimy mass, and I flailed through the shallows. I dropped Katie on the pebbles along the water's edge. Against the bluing flesh of her thin face, I noticed for the first time that she was wearing Paige's lipstick. The shade had blended invisibly before but was suddenly vulgar and bright against her now fading tone.

I had been taught CPR in endless athletic training programs, starting in elementary school, then in high school when I lifeguarded at the club, in college as part of the safety training for athletes, and at an ATP training camp for new professionals. All of that had been done on dolls, though. A latex torso. Katie was not latex.

Somewhere a dog barked, and it awakened me to my own physical condition. I was shaking. I had lost my shoes, and my feet were bleeding, diluted crimson streaks running across the small pebbles back into the pond. I couldn't feel the wounds.

I lowered my mouth to Katie's red lips and, while I was blowing the second breath into her, she vomited into my mouth. I spit the bile back onto her chest. So much adrenaline rushed through me that I threw up some of my own. I flipped her onto her side. Water coursed from between her painted lips and onto the small, mute-colored pebbles until she coughed a tiny sputter, the pond lapping at our ankles. I held on to the girl I had loved since second grade as she shuddered back to life. It was the longest I had held her since our sixth-grade dance. We were silent and animal, gasping the air like it might run out. I almost didn't want to think of Anne, but with Katie in my arms, heaving breath and thrilling on life, she was my only reference. A white dog ran out of the trees, stopped for a moment to look at us, then turned and ran back into the cover.

14

IT WAS AFTER dark. A string of large bare bulbs hung low across the back porch. It smelled like mud and cut grass. Insects whirred unseen in the space around us. Paige had come home from the co-op with cod and potatoes and cherry tomatoes and olives and found us in the bathroom, Katie naked in the bathtub, vomiting into a large empty coffee can. I explained what had happened and found myself glad that I was still soaking wet at the time. Otherwise, I had the brief feeling that Paige wouldn't have believed me, as if I had engineered something untoward. She sat on the floor and administered soft caresses with some secret female tenderness that I could never have summoned appropriately. We ate the cod in the kitchen, standing around the heavy, ancient, and chipped wooden chopping block, Katie laughing everything off.

Afterwards we moved to the porch, drinking from a sweating bottle of cheap, sweet champagne, the kind Anne would have hated.

"I shouldn't have gotten us into that boat," I said.

"You didn't get us in there," Katie said.

"I'm the one that said it would be safe."

"That's not why I got in."

"I should have checked it."

Katie turned to Paige and said, "He used to never do anything like that."

"You mean almost kill you?" I said.

"You *saved* me."

I sighed in pleasure. The champagne bubbled cold against the roof of my mouth. We talked about the TV show *Lost*. About Britney Spears. We spoke none of Anne or Manny or tennis or Kaz. We just drank and laughed and sat in short silences, watching each other, beautiful in the dim light from the gently swinging bulbs. When the champagne ran out, Katie and Paige went to bed, and I reached into the deep pocket of my jacket. I'd seen Kaz write in his notebook a million times, but had never before had any interest. Now I was almost shaking. I lifted it out and laid it on the rusted wrought iron table. There had to be more in this thing than lists of Gatorade. This one little book covered a whole year. I turned to the time before the accident. Kaz's handwriting was feminine and curly. There was no editorializing, just lists of actions, the orchestration of a life recorded so that it could be reenacted when needed. The day before the finals last year, the list of actions ended with one word: ANNE.

The half-moon reflected in the pond, shimmering and breaking into pieces, a pale imitation of the sun's trick from hours before. I held my glass of champagne up to it and said, "Here's to moving on," because I didn't understand what I was feeling, and sometimes, if I can just say what I want to be feeling, it comes to some type of fruition. But this time it didn't seem to help, because I still felt the same, and I looked around to make sure no one had seen or heard me.

Inside, the floorboards creaked and popped as I walked down the dark hallway towards my bedroom, taking extra caution when I passed the guest room. Through a sheer curtain the faint moonlight fell onto an empty bed, still made, covers drawn tight. I stepped in, the floor issuing a high-pitched moan and snap. I lay on the bed, the smell of alien detergent comforting in some strange domestic logic. It was exotic and made me feel rash and left out. I sat up and lifted my champagne to the window. "Here's to not being a giant pussy," I said.

Then I straightened out the sheets, like a giant pussy, and walked down the hallway, rapidly, allowing the floorboards their full range of sound. It sounded like a boat in a storm. I swayed as I walked and stopped at one point with my hand against the wall.

Katie's room was on the far side of the house, adjacent to the kitchen. The door came unstuck from the jamb with a pop, and the old hinges screamed. From the darkness Katie said, "Hello?"

I knocked into a small table on my way to the bed. Papers fell off in a small rush.

"Slow?" Katie said. In the moonlight I could see the other body beside her.

I crawled onto the bed from the foot and lay atop the sheets between those bodies. I said, "Oh God." Arms wrapped around me from both sides. One of them began petting my face. I couldn't even tell whose hand it was. I lifted my arm and placed it over Katie's waist, then buried my face into her neck as more hands ran down my body. A few strands of her hair found their way into my mouth. I bit on them gently, hearing them crunch between my teeth. From behind, Paige petted my head. I was in bed with the woman whom I had loved since I was a boy. I was chewing her hair. I had saved a life. I thought, *What would Manny do in this situation?* He would say something fearless, something that would thrill. So I put my mouth so close to Katie's ear that my lips grazed her skin as I whispered, "You want me to do the monkey-style?"

"What?"

"I said, 'You want me to do the monkey-style?'"

The hands stopped petting my head, and she said, "Manny tell you to say that?"

"I."

She pushed me away.

"I didn't . . ."

111

DOUBLES .....

Katie rolled over, her hair sliding across my tongue and out of my mouth. I looked into the darkness above me, awake, my face warm with blush. Paige slid her hand into mine, and it felt like a lifeline tossed from some dark and unseen shore.

"What?" she said. "Shhhh."

I held on to that sweaty palm. Katie lay with her back to me. The room was silent for what seemed like hours, and I passed into a sickening drunken sleep filled with dreams of drowning.

15

"**I WILL BE** *dog*," Manny said.

I opened my eyes. The air was thick with dust illuminated by sunlight through long yellow curtains. I lifted my head. Manny stood in the doorway of the bedroom wearing a cowboy hat.

"Slow, I will be dog."

Katie sat up, awake and keen in an instant. The sheets fell off of her as she rose. The fine down on her breasts shone in the sunlight just like it did on her jaw. I felt sick with the memory of the night before.

"What are you doing in my house?" she said.

"It's not just yours."

"Yes it is."

"Really?"

"Yeah, it's completely mine."

"What about the car?"

"That too."

"You still shouldn't have stole it," Manny said. Katie stood. The sheet slid off her hips and fell back onto the mattress. A large bruise spread green across a thigh. Small scratches and abrasions were scattered across the fronts of her legs.

"What happened to you?"

She put her hands against his chest and started to push him out of the room. "Slow, it's on," he said as Katie backed him into the hallway.

Paige pulled the covers over her head.

"The duel!"

Katie shut the door.

"The duel!" he said again, muffled now through the door.

Paige slowly sat up and looked around. She was beautiful, her breasts loose and pointy beneath a black tank top.

"Duel?" she said, groggy.

"Oh my God."

I lay back down.

"Just stay here," Paige said. She lay beside me.

Manny called my name from outside.

"Slow!"

I could hear Katie urging him to do something, her voice muffled through the door.

Paige whispered, "Stay."

She touched my thigh. I turned my head to her. The glowing dust seemed to swirl around her backlit face, soft and dark, its features lost to the light. We kissed. The door popped open again, and Manny said, "Slow!"

By the time I turned he was gone.

I dressed and stepped onto the porch. Manny was strapping my bag onto a small luggage rack on the front of a sidecar attached to an orange Honda CB700.

"You've got to be kidding me," I said.

"Can you ask Katie for the bungee cords?"

"Manny, I can't ride in that."

"They're in the kitchen closet."

"Hey!"

"What?"

"I'm not getting in that."

"You have got to face this shit."

"There is no reason I need to get onto a motorcycle."

"You're not going to be on a motorcycle. You're going to be in a sidecar."

"I can't do this," I said. "You don't get it. It was my fault."

"Say what?"

"I broke the brakes."

"On what?"

"The Dart."

"That doesn't mean shit."

"You just hear what I said?"

"If you took the brake pedal and stabbed her in the neck with it, maybe then it would be your fault." He finished securing the bag with the luggage strap and stepped back to admire his work. "Whatever you just said, though"—he shook the bag—"is bullshit. Doesn't have anything to do with anything. You expect me to feel sorry for myself, after coming up here and finding you porking my wife? My wife and my Scarlett?"

"I didn't pork anybody," I said.

"No sir! I'm going to get onto this motherfucking motorcycle and drive down this motherfucking mountain on this motherfucking incredible day. And if you aren't going to come, then you are going to leave a whole bunch of people disappointed, because the duel is on."

He swung a leg over the bike and kicked it, and it roared to life. Another heron appeared overhead, striking a strange silhouette with the *S* of its neck. Maybe it was the same one I'd seen on my walk with Katie. If it was crying out again, I couldn't hear it over the engine. I thought of those hands on my body last night, the secret memory of flesh. I wondered at the thrill Kaz and Anne must have felt in the days after their secret rendezvous. I had done nothing but kiss another woman, and I was already almost drunk with the memory. Anne and Kaz's transgression must have been intoxicating. I envied them.

I looked back into the living room behind me. The old *Times* was still spread across the floor. A bowl of fruit Paige had bought at the co-op sat on the table. I turned my back on it. I couldn't go back in there. Manny held out a white helmet with a black stripe down the middle. I walked to him and took it into my hands. It was cold to the touch, glittering and pocked. I strapped it on. There was a tinted visor, which I flipped down. I thought, *People are going to look at us*. I wanted to be looked at. I got in. The sidecar was surprisingly roomy. As we began to roll down the gravel drive slowly—I couldn't believe Manny was driving slowly, perhaps he had a compassionate bone in that crazy body after all—sunlight flashed on us in dusty bursts through the weave of pine boughs above. I had my helmet on. I had my visor down. Manny began to pick up speed. I wanted him to.

16

THREE FLOODLIGHTS CAST soft yellow orbs onto the grass courts, the light fading to black before the next pool of light edged from darkness into green again. The grandstand was an open bowl glowing at the edge of the grounds. At its entrance, the yellow caution tape was cut. Seating took up only three sides of the court, like the ancient outdoor theaters I'd seen on a tour of Rome the first time I played there. It looked like every player still in town for the tournament was in the stands. Brah, Al Arif, Douglas Adams, Michael DuClos, Tim Kelly, Shannon Ferguson, Gentleman John. Others. ATP officials. There were some people I did not know, mostly young women. And sitting near the net, beside a photographer, drinking coffee from a blue and white paper cup was George Vecsey. Unmistakable, like a Quaker sports minister in his dark suit and wispy beard. Manny told me he'd made some calls. At the time, I didn't know what he meant. Now I knew. If Vecsey wrote anything about this it would be the first time he'd ever used my name in print. A career and it took this.

I walked around the left side of the grandstand, into the darkened walkway, and stopped. I stood there in the darkness, the end of the tunnel glowing ahead of me. I reached my hand to the concrete wall. I had not felt the importance of a tennis match like this in years.

When we were in fifth grade, Kaz's mother arranged a tennis tournament at Ephesus Park. Kaz and I were the only entrants. Her employees were a wall of smiling Asian faces pressed against the chain-link. The sushi chefs, serious and smoking, waifish waitresses, old men in visors and white socks with sandals, they all came to watch. And Kaz's father, running the show, hobbling on that rubber foot from person to person, shaking hands and laughing. I won two games simply by hitting moonball after moonball. It drove Kaz crazy. He just hit them into the net, again and again. I was always smarter. But he was better, even then. He finally got his timing, and the moonballs started coming back. They passed me, hitting corners and skidding off the lines as he won game after game. The set was his at 6–2. It was the last time we'd competed against each other in anything other than a practice set.

I emerged from the tunnel and a spattering of voices from the stands yelled out, their intermittent war whoops rising into the darkness.

Kaz sat in a chair at the edge of the net. Manny stood in the service box and, when I appeared, held one hand into the air. The yelling stopped. From his other hand dangled a bullwhip.

"Ladies and gentlemen!" he said and cracked the whip. "We are here tonight for a tennis duel of the ages, a battle to the death!" He glowed in the thrill of the show, ecstatic to be ringmaster. He spun the whip above his head. "We are here for wrongs to be settled. We are here because Kaz Glover made love to the wife of this man." He cracked the whip in my direction. "His former tennis partner, who has returned from retirement for battle here tonight. Slow Smith!"

Kaz looked worried and unhealthy. His hair was stringy, and in the lights, his skin appeared green. He wore a brand-new left shoe, the other thrown away because of my X. An umpire sat in the high chair. I couldn't believe that Manny had found someone to officiate. I knew the man. He had no chin, a bald head, and drooping pockets for cheeks. He had called our first juniors title in Kalamazoo. I had yelled at him countless times about careless calls. He would agree with anything a linesperson said, whether he was watching or not. Once I saw him pick a bug out of his eye, drop it, then flinch up towards the court to agree with an ace wrongly called out. I wondered at the vacuity of his life, the sad schedule that would allow him time to officiate a grudge match. Maybe his wife lay in a coma; maybe he had lost an unborn child. I looked at him with softness for the first time, a kinship of mediocrity.

From the service line I watched one large moth trace an ellipse in and out of the high lights above. Then I started to count.

One

I had yet to hit a clean serve in close to ten months.

Two

Just that one pink ball sent over the fence at home.

Three

I should have practiced.

Four

Five

Six

Seven

Eight

Nine

I wasn't ready.

One

Two

The crowd was silent, the grandstand buzzing from fluorescent bulbs.

Three

Four

Five

The racquet grip had a small bump in the wrap. I twirled it in my hand, trying to find a hold that avoided it.

Six

Seven

Eight

The official said, "Time. Please."

Nine

Kaz watched my serve pass without even swinging.

My next was another ace.

My third, another.

Then I served it into the net. Fine. I hit a second serve out wide to his backhand. He swung and whiffed. I was invincible.

Douglas Adams was yelling. Manny was yelling. Everyone was yelling. I looked over at George Vecsey and saw that even he was yelling. We switched sides, passing on different ends of the net. I tried to look Kaz in the eye, but he wouldn't meet me.

He served trash, spinning it in, and when I returned his crap down the line and won the first point, he threw his racquet. Usually my edge over Kaz was strategic. So far, though, there had been no need for strategy. I broke his serve at love.

For my next service game, a bit of the pop disappeared from my serve, and the ball came back into play. Kaz was putting more topspin on the ball than I remembered him ever doing before, making it drop late and then rise up to my shoulder on the bounce. He knew me well enough to know that was the thing I hated most. I didn't want him to get comfortable pushing me back with that stuff, though, so at deuce, I rushed the net. He knew what I was doing, it was obvious, and I knew what he was going to do, because that too was obvious. As I closed, he swung low and lifted a topspin lob high into the black space below the lights, into the area where that moth was still orbiting. For a moment they both hovered in air, two yellow spots against the deepest night. It was hard to lob over a man more than six and a half feet tall, but this one would have been easy for a midget. It was tragically short, falling almost directly towards me. I raised my racquet, my arm cocked over my right shoulder. The ball fell further and further away from the moth. I swung, cutting it slightly to make the ball drop. But just like I had with that pink ball on my neighborhood court, I framed it. The ball flew over the net, past Kaz, who spun to watch, past the baseline, and into the stands, towards Brah and a teenage ball girl he was holding hands with. Their hands parted, the girl's flying to her mouth, but not in time to keep the ball from hitting it, a wet splat sounding across the hushed court.

The silence seemed to allow the darkness at the edge of the court to close in. I had never noticed the insects in Queens before, but here they were, pulsing in the space between points, like they had in North Carolina the night Anne had been hit with that motorcycle, and I let my mind leave the court a little. I went back to that January night. "Night Moves." I hadn't heard it since, but I knew that I would somewhere at some time, and it was a moment that I feared, because who knew what restaurant, what elevator I was going to be riding in when I heard Bob Seger next? It was a time bomb, location unknown.

I tried some moonballs. They didn't work. I made that spooky moan, the alien sound of despair.

17

"WHO REMEMBERS AARON Burr?" Manny said. "People respect that you went out there." He was texting while he spoke, furiously poking at his cell phone. "And that was pre-Western. Those guys were like king and queen dueling. Which was also cool. One sec."

He kept punching away.

It was the next morning. I had lost 6–2, 6–0. I had blisters on the ball of each foot. I had a blister on the base of my ring finger. My forearm was so sore it hurt to brush my teeth. My body had softened where it once was callused, had withered where it once was strong. It made me realize that I actually missed Kaz physically. Without him my body was failing.

I walked to the corner bodega to buy a Gatorade, and by the time I returned to Manny's apartment there was a very large woman sitting in one of the plastic chairs in the living room. She looked to be in her late forties or early fifties, though she could have been younger. Light blue makeup shimmered on her greasy eyelids, and she wore a tube-top made of metallic silver nylon. It looked like its seams might rip. It was clear she would have been nearly six feet tall if she stood, and she was thick, just shy of being obese.

She said, "Hey."

"Who are you?"

"I'm with Vinny."

"Who's Vinny?"

"Who are you?"

"Who the fuck is Vinny?"

"This is Vinny's apartment."

"Everything's cool!" Manny called from the bathroom. "Be out in a second!"

"I'll give you guys some private time," I said and walked back down the hallway and onto the street.

There was an internet café three blocks south on Ninth Avenue, down a soulless stretch of New York real estate, an all-American region with a grocery, some trinket stores, an eyeglass retailer, an Amish market, and the business offices for a low-budget horror studio that had hung a cardboard cutout of the Toxic Avenger from the fire escape. He dangled, twirling in the breeze.

Combover had been calling. I had not been answering. There were five emails from him asking me to call him back. The last one said he was worried about his credit card charges. At the cafe I wrote back. "Everything's going great! I'll be back next week at some point. Took Vecsey upstate for a day. Want to stay for the finals this weekend. Made some great connections."

Knowing Manny was making it with the roller derby queen right then made me feel like I was entitled to love. I walked the six blocks to Katie's apartment. I hadn't spoken to her since awakening in her bed after asking if she wanted me to do the monkey-style. I had to talk to her, apologize. It was like poking at a sore tooth. I knew I should stay away, but I couldn't.

When Katie's voice crackled over the brass intercom, I said, "Can I come up?"

The door buzzed, and I passed over the red carpet like I were being drawn inside by a giant magnet. I floated up the stairs. I couldn't get to her fast enough.

Katie wore a green dress and red flats and looked like she was about to go somewhere. Her purse sat on the table beside her, a red jacket draped over the top of a chair.

I said, "I'm an idiot."

"What?"

"Just, just the whole thing."

She waved her hand through the air like it was nothing, then sat on a small white couch, upright and tense. The cushions were hard and surprised me as I sat beside her. She turned away from me, towards the window. The down on the base of her neck glowed from the morning sunlight. I could almost smell suntan lotion. The chlorine. Summers and daylight were her permanent accessories.

"I wasn't acting like myself," I said.

"We're never who we think we are."

"What does that mean?"

She didn't say anything.

"I know who you are," I said.

"Not really."

"Yeah huh."

"I love a woman. That fit?"

"You really think that'll last?"

She continued to look out the window.

"I didn't mean it like that," I said.

She turned and put her hand on mine. I wondered if she knew Paige had kissed me in bed that morning. I felt entitled to their love, a part of the bargain. She looked me in the eyes, and I leaned towards her. She looked down, presenting my mouth with her forehead.

I stood, embarrassed. I didn't know what I was doing.

"I'm sorry," I said. "I'm . . ."

I backed out of her apartment and stumbled down the stairs. I emerged onto Fifty-second Street and felt like everybody was staring. I loved her. She loved a woman. She loved a woman who was walking towards me up Ninth Avenue in a navy blue power suit that shimmered in the sunlight, like a glimmering goldfish shuttling between dull tadpoles. I waved, stunned.

"Hi," Paige said. "You coming from Katie's?"

"I was just getting some coffee."

She looked at my orange Gatorade.

"I heard about last night."

I shrugged.

"I'm sure you were wonderful."

"I wasn't wonderful," I said. "But I'm just glad I went out there. I mean, who respects Aaron Burr? You know what I'm saying."

She furrowed her brow.

"You look great," I said. "Where you going?"

"Work."

"I thought you did acting."

"Translation." Her voice suddenly made sense. "Want to come?"

"To work?"

"They have visitor services."

"Where?"

"The United Nations."

My only other option was returning to Manny and the giantess. I flagged down a cab, and we headed east on Fifty-ninth. Beside me on the plastic upholstery, Paige's purse sat between us, filled with shiny talismans of womanhood—glasses, assorted gleaming plastic tubes of makeup, a dark leather wallet. She said nothing as we inched through the Midtown traffic.

"What language do you translate?" I said as we crossed Fifth Avenue.

"Urdu. But I mostly work with one specific diplomat from Pakistan because he's deaf and I sign."

"You translate into sign language?"

She nodded as if it were obvious.

As a reflex, I almost said, *Deaf? My wife is mostly deaf.* But I didn't want Anne in that cab with us. I just said, "Wow," and watched people pass in a blur until the UN rose out the east side like a giant glass box stuck into the riverbank. For years I had felt so special, that I was the best in the world at something and people should know. I had felt unappreciated. But this beautiful woman beside me translated Urdu into sign language. I felt like anyone was more special than I was.

My UN guide was an intern from Maine, a young woman who actually looked quite a bit like Katie. Refined and dark and thin. She wore a blue suit that also had a sheen. These women all shimmered. Much of the UN did. The colors were all lime greens and pale blues and oranges.

"What do you do?" the tour guide asked me. It took us a while to the get my credentials.

"I work in sports."

"What sport?"

"Tennis."

"My dad loves tennis. Me too, but I'm not very good. It's hard to play in New York."

She led me through long corridors with heavy doors open to bright antiseptic rooms.

"Do you play?" she said.

"Yeah."

"My cousin is a tennis pro outside Bowling Green."

"I play on the tour mostly."

"What tour?"

"The ATP tour."

"What's that?"

"It's the pro circuit."

"Do you know Preston Wittaker? That's my cousin."

"Did he play too?"

"Yeah, he's the pro. Outside Bowling Green."

"I mean I mostly just play tournaments."

"Really!"

"Yeah."

"You ever go to Wimbledon?"

"Eight times."

She stopped walking and looked at me.

"You're a famous tennis player, aren't you?"

"Sort of."

"Who'd you beat at Wimbledon?"

"Last year I beat Aspelin and Perry," I said, which was true. It was a career highlight.

"Who was harder?"

"They're both hard. They're a doubles team. I play doubles."

"I thought you meant *Wimbledon*."

"Yeah, I did."

A short blond man in a sharp blue suit looked at me sharply when I spoke, as if my tone of voice was inappropriate for the hallway. My guide stopped in front of a heavy wooden door and said, "OK. Here we are."

I thought, *I'm never going to talk about tennis again.*

She opened the door to a room decorated with more lime green and orange and pale blue. It was essentially an ornate lecture hall, like those I'd slept in at college, with a dozen rows of empty desks angling down a raked floor towards a small lectern. The room smelled like baby powder. The wall behind the stage was lit with a strange pattern of bare, dim lightbulbs sunk into the wall. To the right of the lectern hung a few displaced continents traversed with golden bands of longitude and latitude. I didn't know which lines were longitude, which were latitude. Surely I had learned at some point in the past, but now they just crisscrossed those landmasses, foreign and magical and unknown.

Behind one podium a man stood beside Paige, his eyes wide above a moustache so black and thick it made me raise my hand to my own upper lip. He cut the air in front of his body into pieces with his hands, pointing, circling, lifting invisible items into the air, spreading fingers on his left hand while pointing at them with his right. It was all so circular. He opened an invisible book and touched a cupped hand to his nose. Then he waited.

Paige! In her shiny suit, she emanated power. I had never thought about why they called power suits power suits. In all my international travel I had never felt so American. She turned from the Pakistani man to a man at a second podium whom I guessed was the American, a man who also looked Pakistani. He was balding and wore rimless glasses perched above his own thick, dark moustache.

She spoke. "Degradation of any prophet is tantamount to defamation of the rest."

"I understand," the American Pakistani said. "But a film is not a political statement."

Now Paige began to gesture. She massaged the air, danced with it. Whether you spoke Urdu sign language or not, her hands clearly indicated that she was speaking softly and precisely. I could hear her accent even in Urdu sign language. The man attached his bulging eyes to that air space, and I wondered if he was used to a message like this being played out before a bosom like Paige's. I guess he must have been if she was his primary contact. She would clearly calm him down.

But no. When she finished he raised his hands into the air like he was releasing two palmfuls of burning rice. He threw the burning rice onto Paige's head. It tumbled down her shoulders and across her power suit. It trickled into her cleavage. She didn't even flinch. She just watched.

Then she turned and said, "We have not taken this lightly. And we are not casting away free speech. But the film will not be released in our country."

"This is a fine line," the American Pakistani said. "A fine line."

Paige turned to the deaf Pakistani and drew a fine line in the air.

I wasn't exactly clear what had just been resolved. Paige disappeared behind closed doors. The handful of people watching trickled out while speaking various languages into their cell phones. Suits and leather attaché cases floated among the seats. I felt like a teenager waiting for my parents to pick me up. After several minutes, Paige opened the door behind me and said, "I'm so glad you waited."

"That was *amazing*."

"Really?"

"I could never do that. I mean, of course I couldn't. But."

"Asad always gets upset."

"You guys were just talking about a movie? At the UN? Is that what this place is for?"

"I just translate," she said. "I can barely remember what we were just debating."

We rode back across the island in a rush, traffic suddenly gone. It seemed we were outside her apartment within minutes.

"Would you care to come in for a cup of coffee?" she said.

I stuck my bottom lip out like Katie and shrugged.

Glittering light blue tiles lined almost every visible surface in her kitchen. Every fixture looked like it cost more than my monthly mortgage payment. There wasn't even a magazine lying on a table, not an apple out of place.

"It's New York," she said as we entered, as if in apology.

She started a gleaming blue enamel Italian coffeemaker on her spotless counter and said, "Mind if I make a call?"

She took the phone into the bathroom and left me to admire her kitchen. I stood at her sink and looked out the window at water towers tilting at different angles across the low buildings. Inside, every fixture sparkled. Outside, rust and decay emerged from standing water on flat rooftops. The blue tile around Paige's sink reflected dim images of me, distorted and dark on the lacquer. I missed my home. The Gatorade left a taste in my mouth like I had been licking aluminum.

Mugs and wineglasses filled the cabinets above her sink. They were all so clean I was scared to use one. I stuck my head under the faucet and drank.

"Can I offer you anything?" Paige said from behind me. I hadn't heard her return.

"I'm a barbarian," I said, wiping my face with my sleeve. The coffeemaker sputtered and hissed as it finished its immaculate process.

"So you were coming from Katie's when I saw you earlier?"

"No."

She tilted her head and looked at me through her eyebrows.

She stepped across the kitchen and just leaned against me. There was nothing to do but put my arms around her. My calloused fingers caught on the shimmery fabric of her jacket. She held on longer than I expected, and when I met her gaze, her face closed in on mine. I was disgusted by the knowledge that I had tried and failed to kiss the last woman who came in this close a contact with me, only an hour or two before. This time it worked. Paige's lips were full and soft, like miniature wet pillows. Nothing like Anne's.

"We can't do this," I said.

"Shhh," she said and kissed me again.

Her flesh was yielding and expansive. Again it reminded me of touching Anne in her final months of pregnancy. I saw all of it.

On her knees on the living room rug Paige rubbed herself, pushing back against me. Sunlight through the open windows lit dust rising around us. We were silent and careful. I let my forehead drop onto her back, then turned my cheek to her skin. Soft moans, too weak to let themselves be heard outside of that flesh, were suddenly audible as I kept my ear to her warm, shifting body. I closed my eyes and thought about how I would remember this. When I opened them, the blue metal door to the apartment was opening. I stopped moving in terror, but Paige continued pushing slowly against me. Katie stepped through the open door. She was still wearing her Christmas colors, the green dress and red flats, and she didn't see us, closing the door behind her like she was entering an empty room. Paige just continued to rub and rock. Then Katie turned. Her eyes met mine. Paige finally stopped moving, and we knelt there, frozen. Katie gasped, one small intake, then turned to the door, opened it, and was gone.

18

THE SUNRISE SLID through refinery towers outside the train window. I closed my eyes and tried to sleep, but kept thinking about what had happened. After Katie had found us, I'd gone back to Manny's. Multiple voices sounded from his closed bedroom, interspersed with flashes of light from under the door. I felt drunk on sin, too near the vicinity of these indulgences. I took my bag and walked to the Victory on Forty-second Street, where I watched *Pirates of the Caribbean II* twice in a row. It made almost no sense the first time I saw it, but by the second, I had begun to see the flaws with even more clarity. Keira Knightly was in it, though, and she was beautiful, and so she made me think of Anne, and of Katie, and of Paige, and of the mess that I had made of everything. The movie ended, and I took a cab to Penn Station, where I bought a one-way ticket on the Carolinian to Durham. It didn't depart until 4:00 AM, so I strapped my duffel bag to my leg and slept intermittently in Grand Central Station, waking in sudden panic of the strange weight attached to myself.

The train was filled with business commuters, all beyond awake, cell phones and the smell of their coffee making the prospect of sleep for me less and less likely. At a stop in New Jersey, a young Mexican woman sat beside me, stuffing a seemingly endless amount of plastic bags full of clothing and food under the seat in front of her. She was emaciated, her teeth were a mess, and her nose bent to the left, but she was young and wearing a dress and was sitting beside me. That's all it took. Again I thought of Anne, Katie, and Paige.

From one of her plastic bags, the woman withdrew a dark oblong fruit that I couldn't identify, which she then began to expertly disassemble with her fingers. She noticed me looking and held part of the fruit towards me. I must have looked more depraved than she did. I took the fruit, but the mechanics of peeling the waxy thing were beyond me.

A man in a blue vest and pillbox hat walked into the car from behind us and began asking loudly for tickets. I guess it was because of Homeland Security, but after every few tickets he demanded identification. I'd ridden Amtrak a lot, and they never checked ID before. Customarily I wouldn't have cared, but today I had purchased my ticket on Combover's Visa. It was his name on the ticket.

"*Buena?*" the woman said.

"Oh. Yeah," I said and began to try to dig my finger into the peel. Juice ran down my forearm as my index finger slid into the pulp. I could feel the Mexican woman's gaze on me as I struggled with the thing.

"Tickets," the man said, close behind us.

I tried to peel the rest of the skin off, starting from the hole, and juice poured into my lap. The engineer appeared beside me.

"Tickets."

I wiped my hands on my pants. I handed him my damp ticket as the woman began to rustle through one of her plastic bags. The engineer glanced at my ticket, then just held it while he waited for the woman. When she finally pulled a folded ticket from a bag, the man said, "ID," and it was clear he would have asked no matter what she handed him. "ID," he said louder. "Identification. You got a driver's license?" He looked down at my ticket, then up at me. "Mr. Como, she got an ID?"

"I don't know," I said. "I don't think she speaks English. She's very nice."

"OK. ID, please. You too."

I gave him my driver's license.

"Mr. Smith, this isn't your ticket."

"That's my boss," I said. "I'm on a business trip, and he bought the ticket for me."

"You can't use someone else's ticket, Mr. Smith."

"OK. Then what do I do?"

"Come on," the man said to the woman. "*Vamos*. Both of you."

In the amount of time it took my neighbor to retrieve all of her plastic bags this guy could have ID'd every stockbroker in the car, but of course they would have all checked out. He had what he was looking for. As we rustled down the aisle, we were interesting enough to make a dozen sets of stockbroking eyeballs leave their BlackBerrys to stare.

Pill Box walked us to the last seating car, where we sat down again, and the woman went through her whole plastic bag routine a second time. She was looking from side to side like a cow in a pen.

"Look," I said to her. "This will be OK."

"*Gracias*," she said, beaming with thanks. "*Gracias*."

I nodded to her, knowingly. But I didn't know anything. I didn't know why I was promising this woman something I couldn't possibly deliver. I held my cell phone up to Pill Box as he passed and said, "Just call my boss. Let's just call him. He'll confirm this."

The man surprised me when he shrugged and said, "OK."

I dialed Combover, and he answered like a wheezing mouse.

"It's about time," he said.

"I need some help."

"Where the hell have you been?"

"I need you to tell this guy I'm on a business trip."

"Why haven't you been calling me back?"

"I've been emailing you. But listen, I need you to help me out."

"With what?"

"Tell this guy it's OK that your name's on my ticket."

"What ticket?"

"Amtrak."

"Why's my name on your ticket?"

"I bought it with your credit card."

"I never said you could buy tickets."

"How was I going to get home?"

"You said you had a ride."

"Only up here."

Pill Box reached for the phone. I let him take it. Before he could even pace to the end of the car and back, he closed it and shook his head, the plastic rim of his hat pointing from eastern refinery to western refinery.

This was no organized reception, no intricate capture. It was simply a catch and release. At the DC exit, they removed us from the train.

The station in DC was grand. Three-story marble arches vaulted over the low-budget travelers confined to the rails and the businessmen who passed by the throngs of nobodies, the mystery fruit–eating Mexican women and destitute retired doubles tennis players.

The Mexican woman walked away, and I waved, expecting her to turn around and remember that she needed my help, but she didn't. It was like she had expected this very sequence of events to happen from the moment she'd boarded the train. From one side of a slotted Plexiglas window I said, "I need to buy a ticket with this Visa, but my name needs to be on it."

The attendant swiped the card. She swiped again.

"You have another card?" she said.

I called Combover again. He answered immediately.

"I know what you've been doing," he said. He sounded tired and resigned.

"What do you mean?"

"Vecsey wrote about you."

"Where?"

"*Tennis*."

"The new issue isn't even out yet."

"Online. You can't spend our money on whatever it is you're up to, Slow. I want to help you. I do. But I don't have any money, man. I can't believe you've put me in this position."

"It's not what you think."

"You're going to have to buy your own ticket home."

"Look who wrote the article. Vecsey! Who did I say I was with?"

"I'm sorry."

Anybody else would have just bought their tickets with their own money. But ATP health insurance was dependent upon how much you bought into it. Which meant for me, it was crap. My measly pittance from Combover had left me with less money than I had had when I was eighteen years old. After the last round of medical bills had been paid, I probably had $200 in my bank account. Maybe less.

I searched my phone for Adam Lawler's phone number. He was one of those classmates from Durham Academy who had been in my life since nap time in kindergarten. Even our dreams had shared the same vicinity for years. Now apart, we stayed in touch like we were never far away. He lived in DC, was in training for the CIA. At least that's what we all thought. He said it was high-security State Department work, but ever since he started, friend after friend had been called by government security agents, who met them in Starbucks, living rooms, empty conference rooms asking details about Adam's past. No one had called me, but if they had I could have told them that he was a perfect candidate for the job, that since he was a young boy he had read weapons manuals, had painted his face black and hid in the bushes beside the golf course, and obsessed over Tom Clancy novels and spy movies. He endeavored to reinforce stereotype. He had attended West Point. He had red hair cut into a tight flattop. He loved Guinness. In fact, he loved everything that had alcohol in it. He answered his phone before the first ring had finished sounding.

"Adam Lawler!" he said.

"I need evacuation."

"Slow?"

"Yeah," I said, "I just got kicked off the Amtrak."

"Seriously?"

"Yeah."

"That's awesome."

He picked me up in a golden Ford Explorer with a disassembled Ping-Pong table in the back.

"You look terrible," he said as I placed my bag on top of the Ping-Pong table. I explained what had happened with the ticket. I left out the phone call to Combover.

"I'm starving," I said.

"You want a cigarette?"

"I mean for food."

"You like empanadas?"

"I guess."

"When I was in Rio last summer, all we ate was empanadas."

"Rio?"

"It was a language study."

He drove tight on the bumper of a taxi, leaving a yard of air between us.

"So there's this empanada place in my neighborhood," Adam said as the taxi came to a stop. We cut into a Texaco and drove through the lot at full speed, compressing and releasing the Ford's shocks in an instant as we crossed the curb. The service bell rang behind us as we rumbled into the road. Adam didn't ask about my trip.

The restaurant was a fluorescent glass storefront on the corner of a block where the steps of brownstones receded up a hill into darkness. The workers made me wonder what had happened to the Mexican woman with the bags. Adam told me about Rio while I ate a spinach empanada.

"I thought you already spoke Spanish," I said.

"I do."

"Then what were you studying?"

"Portuguese. They speak Portuguese there." Chewing a mouthful of empanada, he looked at me like I was an idiot. In some of the places I played, I never even spoke to a local unless they were working at the hotel or driving us to a court. And even then, I didn't pay attention. I was usually on my phone, reading a magazine, or zoning out to music. It is important when you travel as much as we did that you do not engage in every new destination, but rather keep your own world constant, insular, and distinct. Adam went on. "And we kept our eye on some of the favela violence a little, too. But that's mostly narcotics." He often told me things like this, things that spoke of a wide underworld, unknown and vast. "And there was this girl," he said, "who looked like Molly Ringwald. Brazilian. Ever notice how Molly Ringwald's mouth always hangs open?"

I had not. I devoured three spinach empanadas. Adam recommended the chicken. "Spinach is for vegetarians," he said. I drank two Pacificos. I was thrilled to be out of New York, away from Kaz, removed from anyone who knew about what he had done with my wife.

Adam lived up a dark hill behind the restaurant in a basement apartment of one of the shadowed brownstones. The venetian blinds on the one window facing the street were closed with the authority of having been in that position for months. A three-foot television monopolized the living room, surrounded by mounds of DVDs. An L-shaped leather couch stretched across two walls, the coffee table covered in *Wall Street Journals* and gun manuals. Above the couch hung two framed prints of West Point. I helped him set up the Ping-Pong table in an extra bedroom furnished with nothing other than one desk lamp sitting on the carpet, its green lampshade tilted upward, revealing the hard, bright edge of a lit lightbulb.

Ping-Pong. Gin. Vodka. Coors Light. A walk for more empanadas. I could barely stay awake. I lost track of how many Ping-Pong games I won in a row. It felt wonderful to dominate. I hit Adam in the forehead with the ball twice. I beat him left-handed. We were pouring sweat. My body felt like it was shutting down. Before I fell asleep on the couch, Adam showed me pictures of the Brazilian. Her mouth was shut. As I drifted off, the monolithic muted television flashed CNN, seeping red in surges through my heavy, closed eyelids.

I awoke wet. I reached into my crotch. The liquid was not urine. The leather beneath me was slippery with it. For a moment I was sure someone had spilled a large amount of water on me, but then I realized how hot I was. It was sweat. In the bathroom I vomited until I was left with nothing, bending over the toilet with thin strings of saliva dangling from my chapped lips. I couldn't believe I had done this to myself. I changed spots on the couch and wrapped the damp blanket around me. In the extreme air-conditioning, my flesh recoiled from the fabric. Back in the bathroom, I filled the toilet again, this time with frothing diarrhea. I shook, then pulled the trash can in front of me and heaved nothing into it.

I put on dirty dry clothes from my bag and lay on the couch, shaking. I longed to turn off the television but could not find the remote. I passed in and out of sleep. I vomited more. I bled from the application of so much toilet paper. I'd never had a hangover like this. Something was terribly wrong. For one fever-induced hour, I convinced myself that I had contracted malaria from years in my swamp of a neighborhood.

At dawn, Adam passed through in a freshly pressed suit, carrying a newspaper and coffee. Dim sunlight exploded into the room as he opened the door. He closed it behind him without even looking at me. I tried to focus. Pictures of fields of spinach flashed on the television, interspersed with CNN anchormen. I crawled to the television and turned it up at the source.

Wolf Blitzer said, "The hospitalization of dozens of people across the country has been attributed to the tainted spinach."

I had been poisoned by empanadas. I shook in the bathroom again, showered in a state of rapidly fluctuating temperature. There was nothing that might help. I checked the kitchen. It was filled with beer cans and specialty pastas, olives, and a number of jars of artichoke hearts. I walked outside, down the hill, trying to gauge the amount of time before I would need a toilet. My head was splitting. I found a corner bodega and bought Ritz crackers and Bayer. The discovery made me briefly euphoric.

With daylight I settled into a rhythm of shaking, going to the toilet, and sleeping. I thumbed through the weapons manuals piled in a basket by the edge of the couch. I watched the only movie I could find that wasn't a James Bond film. *Spies Like Us*. Adam's apartment confirmed everything. He was a caricature of himself.

In a moment of desperation I called Combover. On his voice mail I said, "Steve, it's Slow. I'm in DC. I got spinach poisoning. I gotta get home, man. This was a business trip. It really was."

It was almost impossible to discuss my sickness with Adam when he returned. "That sucks" and "oh man" was all we could say. We were incapable of investigating empathy. We were schooled only in personal destruction. He said, "I told you you shouldn't have gotten the spinach. Want to get a drink with me and some friends?"

"Seriously?"

"It'll be good for you."

I wanted a doctor. A trainer. I wanted Anne. She would have brought me tea and crackers and made me get into a hot bath or a cold bath. Whichever was appropriate. I didn't know. I longed for her. I sipped water, which then trickled out of me in various ways. More dry dirty clothes and then *The Color of Money*.

CNN covered spinach like it was a terrorist attack. Two children died. I wondered if, when I died, they would mention me on CNN. Former tennis player Slow Smith dies due to poison spinach. I doubted it. Another night of diarrhea and shivers. My head hurt so bad that I cried. Again Adam exited healthy with confidence at dawn.

I awoke in the afternoon to knocking on the door and crawled to it with the blanket wrapped around me. I opened it, the sunlight an electrical shock to my brain. Fever had never induced hallucinations before, but for a moment I questioned whether or not what I was seeing was real. I was looking at Kaz. He was clean-shaven, and his hair had been cut into a bristly crop. His fingernails were perfect.

He said, "Combover called me."

It must have only taken a couple phone calls for Kaz to figure out where I was. He knew who I knew in DC. He stepped inside and sat with his back to the window, a silhouette before the drawn blinds. He had gone heavy on the aftershave. The aroma made my stomach turn. I had eaten nothing but crackers in more than a day. I was drained in every possible way. I let the silence ripen.

"Let me take you home," he said.

"You serious?"

"I want to apologize."

"I'm not going anywhere with you."

"What can I do?"

It was a question I couldn't answer. What I wanted from him was all in the past. I wanted him to not sleep with my wife.

I sighed. "Tell me what happened."

"Slow."

"Tell me."

He didn't speak for a long time. I felt nauseated for a moment but breathed softly and shallowly until the vomit lowered itself back into the last safe area of my stomach.

"It happened in New York."

"Last year?"

He nodded. "After charades."

"Who started it?"

"I'm not going to go into detail, man."

"You guys do it without a condom?"

He didn't look up. I could feel the vomit beginning to rise.

"Now this one's important," I said. "You do it without a condom? Hey!" He looked up. It was the most energy I had expended in days.

"This isn't smart, Slow."

"She kissed you," I said. "Then you kissed her. Then what, you started groping each other? She put her hands in your pants? She took her clothes off? One of you probably said, 'What are we doing?' Or 'We can't do this.' But you did it. Am I right?" I shook my head. "You know what happens when people have sex? You know what the outcome can be? The miracle of life?" I was floating, high on spinach fever. "Yeah. That happened."

"We didn't . . . ." Kaz said. "OK?" He held up one open hand. "What Anne and I did was wrong. We knew that. She knew that. But I know what's been going on with you and Katie and Paige. So you're doing this stuff with Katie and Paige—no, just listen. And in the end, we're all good people. We are. We're good and we're bad. You too. Just wait! We all love each other too much. I'm serious, I think we all love each other so much that we've messed everything up. Because I love you, man. And I'm not going to lie to you. We didn't use a condom. She didn't want me to."

The blanket fell off of my shoulders as I stood. I took the two steps to Kaz and then vomited onto the side of his face.

part

2

19

OVER THE TOP of my computer, I watched my officemate put a hand on the back of his head and twirl one finger into an area of hair that was only a few inches long and stood out at strange angles like it had been caught in a paper shredder. For weeks I couldn't make sense of the hairstyle until I finally realized that it was not a style. It was from him pulling his own hair out. He wound one hair around his finger, then yanked. He held it in front of his face, said, "I know!" into the phone, and dropped the hair onto the carpet. He covered volleyball, field hockey, gymnastics, and softball. Track-and-field, crew, and tennis were mine. We worked for the university. The Combover incident had made me look elsewhere for work, and in truth, this wasn't a better job. It was more of the same, handling sports information, emailing dates and phone numbers and stats and quotes. I had been here for three months. He continued to talk, and so I opened Steve G Tennis—a website that gathered every tennis result and statistic—and started reading the names of friends.

Sixteen months had come and gone since Anne had gone into the hospital, sixteen months since I had filed for my protected ranking. Anne was still in the hospital, but the ranking was now unlocked. It gave me eight chances, eight tournaments to sign in with the same ranking points I'd had a year ago. I'd used my first option two weeks earlier when I'd flown to Baton Rouge by myself, signed in, and took what came to me. Nick Jones. A twenty-nine-year-old American with short dreads who had been on the tour for seven years and still had only two points to his name. To other players he was an ancient joke, and I was one year older than him. We lost in the first round. I got my check for $70 and got back on a plane the same day I'd arrived. I felt like I had played a different game than the one I had once made my living at. It wasn't my strokes, my legs, or my volleys. It wasn't even Nick, who had actually played well. It was that Nick wasn't Kaz. I felt lost on court without him.

I was searching for my own name in the rankings when the phone rang. I flinched. It almost never rang.

"Sports Information," I said. "Slow Smith."

"This is Dr. Julia Green," a young woman said. I barely registered the woman's voice, my attention instead focused on the fact that Kaz had lost 1 and 3 in qualifying at Estoril. He had signed in with DP Burris? I couldn't imagine what circumstances had led to that pairing. Burris, who had beaten Roddick in juniors in '91 and been going downhill since. I had been watching Kaz's progress for months. His ranking had been plummeting, racking up results like Estoril with partners not even as good as Burris. I had the feeling he was just as lost on court as I had been with Nick.

The woman on the phone said, "Hello?"

"This is Sports Information," I said. We often received misdirected calls from the main switchboard, and this repetition of error had made me almost immune to the voice of another over the phone. The woman's voice grew muffled as she spoke to someone else in the room. Then she said, "Your wife would like to talk to you."

"This is Sports Information."

"Slow Smith?"

"Uh."

"Your wife is Anne Smith?"

"Yes?" I looked away from the Steve G.

"OK. Hold please."

I did have a wife. It suddenly occurred to me that this call was for me. I had the momentary impulse to place the phone back on its base. Then, with no regard for my desire to pace, Anne said my name. There was no zombie tenor, no wavering slur. Her voice sounded exactly the same as it always had.

"Slow?" she said. "Hello?"

"Anne?"

My officemate plucked another hair and then, holding it aloft, turned to me and stared.

"Where are you?"

"Anne?"

"Yes! Where are you?"

"At work."

"Work?"

"Yeah," I said. I even laughed.

"What do you mean?"

"It's."

"What happened?"

"Where are you?"

"I'm . . . at the hospital?"

"Are you alright?"

"What happened?"

"We had an accident."

"Can you come?" she said. She sounded confused and half-asleep.

"I'll be there in a second."

My hands shook on the steering wheel. It was a 2002 Volvo wagon. I sped onto Franklin Street, dodging the afternoon traffic. I couldn't understand the rules of the road. I didn't know when to stop, when to go. I pulled into the parking lot of the art museum to breathe. There was a large sculpture of a horn in the lawn, lifted into the air on two small poles, with a pedestal at the small end. I remembered walking across that small expanse of grass with Anne before a gala at the museum one summer evening. I was in a tuxedo, she in a long golden dress from the '30s. The curator's husband had asked her if she was going to the Oscars. I let go of her hand and stood on that pedestal and whispered "This is your conscience" into the small end of the horn. My voice emerged amplified from the other end, secret and metallic, audible even to Anne.

In the bathroom off the hospital lobby, I turned on the hot water and let it run. The fluorescent lighting shone directly on my bald spot. I don't know how much it had thinned since I'd last seen her. I was heavier. Paler. I had grown a thin beard. Steam crept up the mirror, slowly erasing my aging reflection. I washed my hands, rose up the elevator, crossed the ICU, and looked at the humans. I'd seen them all before. They were wired to machines, inflated by tubes, fed in drips; paralyzed processors of liquid. For sixteen months Anne had been one of them, every day of it on film. The Polaroid ritual made me feel like I was in control of the situation, that nothing could happen without my knowledge. But of course, it could. It had. Something else was in charge, something that made Anne wake up that afternoon for no apparent reason other than it was just time. When I pulled aside the curtain in her doorway she turned her head to look. Still greasy and thin, her hair was tucked behind each ear now. Something so simple, clearly placed by her own narrow fingertips, made her more recognizable than she had been in months. I put a hand to my own hair, embarrassed of my aging body. I kissed her withered lips. They felt like wrinkled plastic. She kissed back nonchalantly. She didn't know how long it had been since I had last kissed her and received a response. Then she put her hands under the sheets. I imagined her feeling the ridge of the scar from where they had cut her open. It had already healed.

I looked around. Wasn't there a doctor here? The knowledge of the child's death seemed beyond my jurisdiction. I couldn't believe they'd left me alone with my own wife.

"What happened?"

I told her. About the motorcycle, about the baby. Even about Bob Seger. I told her everything but that I had fouled the brakes. It was the first time in close to a year I had recounted the accident in detail. "Here," I finally said and lifted from the bedside table a BNP Paribas tote bag from a hospitality basket at the French Open. It was now with Polaroids. She took it from me, but the weight of the bag was too much for her withered limbs. She dropped it. Two photos fell onto her chest. She picked one up and gazed at it with wonder. She ran her finger over the corner, pressing on the sharp edge. I was afraid her paper skin might tear. The date read January 6, 2006. More than two months earlier.

"This is what I look like?" she said, raising a finger to her hair.

"Not exactly."

"Let me see the rest."

Anne had always been prone to long silences. I watched the side of her head as she looked at photo after photo. If she viewed each for this long it would take all week. After five more photos, she started to cry so hard that I was scared she would hurt herself. I worried her atrophied muscles wouldn't be strong enough to maintain it. A nurse came into the room and then left quickly without doing anything. I sat on the edge of the bed, apprehensive of Anne's fragile body, scared to hold her.

She said, "Did you take one today?"

"Not yet."

She lifted the camera from the bedside table and, with more effort than I would have ever expected—as if lifting a small barbell—she handed it to me.

Through the viewfinder the hospital room was a new landscape, transformed by life. The turquoise sheet was pushed down to Anne's waist. Her white gown made the frame glow. Her face was a wet, red, inflated rind. And when the flash filled the room, I was aware that, for the first time in almost a year and a half, it blinded a second pair of eyes. They were spooky and blue and open and wet and looking right at me.

20

ATTENDING TO HER bedsores, watching nurses massage her withered limbs, my motivation to tell Anne what I had learned disappeared. But she knew me too well. One afternoon she lifted the camera from her crowded bedside table and held it to an eye. She said, "Tell me what you've been thinking about."

"I don't want to do this."

She sighed. "OK. Here, I will."

She handed me the camera, and I raised it with dread. It had been a long time since I'd looked at Anne through the viewfinder with this specific fear, this apprehension of revelation.

"The dress that you gave me for Christmas last year?" she said. "They didn't lose it at the cleaners. I dropped it in the clothes bin up at the Texaco on 54."

The flash was still fading in my eyes as film whirred out of the camera. It wasn't this past year. It was the one before. She had lost the last one. But the year before, yes. That was the first time I had ever bought clothing for my wife. We had always had the agreement that it was just something we wouldn't do. I had no idea what size she was, where I might even shop for her. But one night she had opened a JCPenney catalog on the couch and said, "Pick the outfit on this page that I might wear." It was a game she was fond of playing with her girlfriends. They would gasp in laughter and disgust, turning to a page filled with high-waisted jeans, asking each other to guess which they would choose if forced. To my surprise that night, I unerringly picked what Anne would want. It seemed I had crossed an aesthetic divide. A few days later I saw my neighbor wearing a dress that I complimented her on. "Dan picked this out for me," she said, smoothing it across her thighs. I thought, *I can do that.*

I didn't know what I was looking for in TJ Maxx, but when I found a red dress with a black tie around the waist, I bought it. Anne opened it on Christmas morning and said, "You bought this for me?"

"You hate it."

"Let me try it on."

The dress fit perfectly. From time to time I would see it in the closet and wonder if she would ever wear it. Then it was gone. Now I knew why.

"Alright," I said. "I'll tell you what I was thinking about."

Just then a nurse with large thighs in tight pink scrubs entered the room and whispered, "I need to look at your tube."

"What?" Anne said, turning to the nurse and looking at her through the viewfinder.

"Your tube."

"What?" she said. She lowered the camera.

"She's hard of hearing," I said.

"Your nose tube!"

The tube in Anne's nose had mashed her nostril to one side for so long that when the nurse took it out the nostril actually stayed in its malformed position. Anne's body was like this in so many ways, alive and alert but still failing. It had for too long been dormant. The doctors said that the path back to health was fractured, unclear, and difficult. The nurse rubbed lotion onto the flattened flesh, and Anne winced as it entered a small red crack. I held her hand as she sucked air through clenched teeth.

"Fuck. It burns," she said.

I squeezed her hand.

"Tell me what you were going to say," she hissed.

"I can't remember."

"Come on. Eeeeeshhhhhhh."

"It was just about some movie."

My courage left with the nurse. It didn't matter what Anne had done. I just wanted her nose to go back to normal.

The next morning, she picked up the camera and said, "Tell me that thing."

I shook my head. "I told you."

"Alright. Take another one of me, then."

I lifted the camera to my eye in terror. It was like I was driving slowly towards a brick wall. I knew the collision was imminent but did nothing to stop it. The flash exploded as she said, "I didn't put up any of those fliers for Winnie."

"You told me you put them up," I said pathetically.

"I hid them under the carpet in the office. In the back, near the arrow lamp."

"Why?"

"Fliers never work. Let me see the picture."

I handed her the developing image, and she silently watched herself emerge from the depths.

"See." She held it up. It looked like all of the others. "This is an amazing picture."

Winnie was our cat who, after eight years of quality, consistent love, disappeared one afternoon after walking into the woods. When I got home, I lifted the carpet in the office and there, underneath, covered in dust, was Winnie looking back at me. Later that night, Anne's lungs began to fill with liquid. By the time I returned they had moved her back to the ICU.

She said, "What if I don't make it?"

"You'll make it."

"You always look down when you lie."

"I'm not lying."

I looked down.

"Where's Kaz been?"

Her breath gurgled in her chest. I put my head in my hands and listened to her gurgle. I just let her gurgle and gurgle and gurgle.

"OK," she finally said and picked up the camera.

"I don't want to take this picture."

"Please."

It was like she was rushing, afraid she wouldn't have another chance. She put the camera to her eye.

She said, "Tell me what you know."

"This isn't my secret."

She continued to look at me through the camera.

"I know about you and Kaz," I said.

The film whirred out the front of the machine as the flash died.

One

Anne lifted her twig of an arm to the camera and plucked the developing fruit.

Two

Silence filled the room dangerously, like water rising quickly. If she didn't say anything else before nine, I was leaving.

Three

Her parents still lived in town. I wasn't the only one who had been visiting, been waiting for her to awaken. She had a sister in Raleigh. There were people who had known her longer than I, the woman out of whose womb she had wriggled cold and viscous and crying.

Four

I wondered if, when she had had the baby, if it would have looked

Japanese. There was no sustainable lie in that equation. Their affair was timed for destruction.

Five

I stood at the window and watched a storm cloud darken the horizon, so solid and heavy it looked like a mountain range had suddenly risen out of Burlington. A man in a brown suit pushed an elderly woman across the parking lot in a wheelchair, maneuvering around a boy skateboarding, the clacking of his board against the pavement like a brash announcement of youth floating up and through the window pane. A petite young nurse sat atop a low brick retaining wall grown over with kudzu and smoked a cigarette.

Six

Someone entered the room behind me and punched several buttons on a machine before leaving, the electronic beeps punctuating the silence like an ice pick through a lampshade.

Seven

"If you don't have anything else to say then I'm going to leave," I said.

Eight

I turned. The bag was open on Anne's chest, dozens of Polaroid Annes spread across her turquoise torso, sleeping and frozen and small. And then, in one rectangle near her left hand, I recognized myself. It was the photo she had just taken. I was just as pale, bloated, and bald as I had been in the bathroom mirror. But there was an electricity and thrill in my eyes. I saw Anne's coveted moment of truth. I looked more alive than I had in months.

Nine.

21

THERE WERE DAYS I had imagined I wouldn't speak to Anne once she awoke. There were nights when I dreamt we would make love in the hospital bed. Mostly I envisioned scenes of groveling and tears. Moments of profound understanding of the pain she had caused. But at no point had I thought she would be the one who wouldn't apologize. Things happened for a reason, I suppose, and Anne wasn't one to deny the cause or the effect. Watching her will her body back to the world of the living, I knew that my pain wasn't the only pain in the room. I should have been groveling too. She was in that bed because of me. Because I couldn't attach a simple brake pedal. But I could see how her physical pain might heal. There were machines and doctors and pills. The cure to my injury started on her tongue, and she wasn't speaking. I was jealous of my insult, possessive of my ache.

The next morning I called her mother. I had not slept or eaten and knew that I sounded like a crazy person. I said, "Your daughter had an affair before the accident, and I tried to talk to her about it, but she won't."

Her mother was a registered nurse who had not worked in more than a decade. She was sweet and enjoyed her obese cats and her very clean house and her large collection of modern art, and she had always been lovely to me and appreciative of the fact that I had married her daughter.

"I know," she said.

I sighed. It was a cliché. Everyone but I had known.

She said, "She's not a good communicator."

"I," I said. "I can't do this. I can't keep going there every day. Not now. I'm sorry."

I finally fell asleep on the couch, but after twenty-five minutes the phone rang, and I jerked awake on the couch. Drool wet my cheek. Before I picked up the phone, I spoke into the empty room. I said, "Hello. Hello. Hello. Hello. Hello. Hello. Hello." I wanted to clear the sleep out of my throat before I finally said the word to another human. Then I picked up the phone and said it again. "Hello."

It was Anne's father. He was the museum director, but he seemed to come more from the business world than the art one. He was a short man with a shock of thick, bristly black hair. All of his coworkers were women, and I had wondered if that made him harder or softer. I could never decide which. I felt like he knew I had just practiced my greeting, that he could hear the deception.

He said, "I understand there're some complications here."

"Yes, sir."

"Not enough reason to end a marriage."

"It's not that."

"Looks that way to me."

I wiped at my cheek and let a moment of silence play out on the phone line. The sun had angled through a gap in the limbs and lit the room with an intensity that appeared only a few minutes each day, a revelation of dust and shadow and color. I had to squint inside of my own living room.

"She's going to have to move in with us. Diane will take care of her, I suppose."

I grunted.

He said, "Diane had an affair, when we were young." Anne's father had never before disclosed even the slightest bit of personal information to me.

"I didn't know."

"Well, neither does Anne. And I'm going to trust you not to tell her. But it's true, and afterwards I imagine I felt a bit like you do right now. And I left, for a little while. I did. I moved into the YMCA. You know what that taught me?"

"No, sir."

"That the YMCA stinks. But also that I had to put my ego on hold. That a marriage isn't just about my ego. I had to humble myself to make it work. Do you understand what I'm saying? You're going to have to humble yourself."

I knew there was a truth there, but I wanted to ask him if he didn't think this was already humbling enough. I wanted to ask him if Diane had conceived their daughter during the affair, if the affair had been with his best friend and business partner. If he had had to retire from his profession to tend to her. I wanted to say, *All affairs aren't the same.* But I had a feeling I knew what he would say. That it still wasn't enough. That all affairs have two sides. But this one was mine, and I had begun to hold it dear. I couldn't say that I didn't still love her. I did. But I felt like forgiveness was the wrong thing to do. This hurt required respect.

Over the next few weeks I used my vacation leave to enter six more tournaments, adding myself on to sign-in sheets as a partner to unmatched players, names only vaguely familiar to me from the bottom of the rankings sheets on Steve G, names looking for another name to add beside them just so they could get into the draw and play. I went to Cairo, Mexico City, two futures in Florida. I went to Africa twice.

While I was in Florida the second time, Anne's father sent movers to the house to take the items I'd marked with yellow Post-it notes. In a letter I had already explained all they should take, but the Post-it notes were for additional clarity. I wanted whoever came into the house to be certain: They could take almost everything.

I lost in the first round of each tournament. By March, I had one protected entry left. After that, my points were gone. I needed to win. And when I played Forest Hills with Kaz, I won. So on March 12, when the last of the winter had dissipated from the North Carolina air, I bought a ticket to New York City. Because I was going to go to Forest Hills. And I was going to play with Kaz. And I was going to win.

22

THE SUBWAY ROSE above ground as it neared Queens, sunlight filling our car, illuminating the graffiti scratched into the windows. The orange and yellow seats glowed. The only other people on the train, a teenage Puerto Rican couple, put on large white sunglasses and held on to each other like they might fall out of the seat. At unsaid intervals they kissed, groping each other's necks.

At Forest Hills I left the teenagers bumping sunglasses. People on the sidewalk all seemed to be decades older and extremely healthy. They strolled past in summer scarves and sweaters, carrying newspapers, shopping bags, and very large drinks. This crowd made it seem like youth was a just a hassle and that they were all glad to be done with it.

At the clubhouse, out of some reverse imprinting, I wiped my own hands on my chest as I passed the woman at the desk. She did the same. I walked past the photo of Connors with his Wilson T2000, past Bill Tilden in long white pants, past those tennis-playing women in layered dresses frozen in frames on the wood-panelled walls, past the picture of me and Kaz, and upstairs to the lounge.

The ancient volunteer at the sign-in desk had a narrow, bald head with large ears that weren't doing a very good job of holding up a pair of thick metal-frame eyeglasses. He held them on to his face with one finger as he leaned over to see whom I was signing in with. The blank beside Kaz's name was still blank. For a brief moment I pitied him, that the other players had all already seen this. There wasn't even a new kid who would take this chance. But I wasn't a new kid.

"When's sign-in end?" I said.

The man looked at his watch.

"Nine minutes. No." He squinted. "Seven minutes. What does your watch say?"

"It's OK," I said and wrote SLOW SMITH onto the paper.

The man said, "You two won this thing before, yeah?"

I set the pen down and nodded.

I felt the sidelong glances when I returned that afternoon to see the draw. Kaz and I were up first after 10:00 the next morning. I made sure not to look at other brackets. Projecting the next round was bad luck. Still, it was hard not to notice the Simon brothers. They were sitting not six feet away, staring. I didn't keep up with shifts in the top rankings, who was number 3 or 5 or anything like that. It didn't make any difference. But the Simon brothers were at the top. That much I was sure of. Number 1 and 2. They were both younger than I, wore short blond goatees, and made the sign of the cross when they won. They were some of the nicest and most talented players on the tour, and I harbored a deep disgust with almost everything they said or did. Anne always called them "the dudes." They appeared in a Visa commercial once, the only doubles players ever to land a television spot. In it, they polished steam off a locker room mirror, revealing their almost identical faces as a voice said, "One family. One game. One goal. One card. Visa." I saw it with my mother once, and the depths of envy I felt left me embarrassed and ashamed.

It was rare and in many ways frowned upon for top players to attend a challenger tournament, which was a tier below the top tour events and was what Forest Hills had been since they started hosting professional play again in 2000. But I knew that Sandy, the taller and older of the brothers, had recently had an ankle sprain, and so I guessed they were slumming it here for practice.

When Kaz walked in he didn't see me. He said something to Maxwell Council, a young black American who had a diamond in each ear, then slapped him on the back and laughed. Maxwell did not laugh back. He just stared. Kaz turned to follow his gaze. People began to leave the room like a silent order had been given.

I had not seen Kaz since he'd surprised me in DC. His nails were still trimmed. His hair was still short and clean. There was no facial hair. He said nothing, just looked at me. I knew what I looked like. Losing had made Kaz look better. Not so with me. Sleep had come only in spells of a few hours at a time for months. Dark bags hung under my eyes, and I hadn't gotten more than a few hours' sun since napping in my yard on a warm afternoon in February.

"What are you doing?" he said.

"Winning this tournament."

He looked at the draw sheet, then raised one of his manicured hands to his mouth. He pulled at his nose. The announcer for the soccer match on the television continued to yell in Spanish.

"You serious?" he said.

I nodded.

He looked at me deeply, something he didn't often do, then said, "You have my book?"

I unzipped my tennis bag and lifted his diary from between racquets. He took it from me, then flipped through the pages until he stopped at one and squinted.

"OK. Tonight we eat chicken teriyaki at Teriyaki Boy. On Ninth Avenue. 7:23."

I said, "This is so stupid."

Kaz had always been the one to invest in the superstitious reenactment of routine. I had just played along. But now I was the one who had combined the parts of this supernatural equation. I had the promise of surety in what we would be doing for at least the next day. I had the knowledge of what I would eat, with whom, and when and where I had to be in the morning. I knew with whom I would have to warm up and on what end of which court I would be doing so. As I left the room, the television announcer yelled, "Goal!" in one bizarre, drawn-out scream.

Kaz filled four small paper cups with ginger sauce and sat. He opened his diary, read a line, then got up and returned to the condiment selection, where he filled one more. He dumped them all onto his mound of steaming rice.

"Tomorrow morning, we have to eat everything bagels with cream cheese and chives at that bagel place near the subway," Kaz said, shoveling rice into his mouth, smacking so loud that a couple beside us turned to stare.

I already knew, I already knew. It had been reenacted so many times. But as far as I knew, there was no scripted exit from this meal. So I set down my fork and stood. My voodoo quota had been met.

"We done here?"

He looked at my empty plate and shrugged. As I walked away, he said, "Nine o'clock! And wear black socks!"

When I hit Ninth Avenue I half-expected Manny, Katie, or Paige to appear. But I hadn't told anybody I was here, and I wasn't going to. I pulled my hood over my head and hurried to the subway.

The next morning, as Kaz chewed his bagel, I watched a small dollop of cream cheese bounce as it clung to the bottom of his chin. He couldn't take the silence. "Where you been living?" he said. One chive dangled precariously out of the cheese. I just watched, amazed at the physics of cream cheese. "OK," he said, giving up on a response. Then he leaned forward, presenting his chin. "Get it."

I looked around. One young woman in a headscarf stood at the counter, an elderly couple behind her each with a large Banana Republic bag. They weren't watching, so I did what I knew I had to do. I took my napkin and wiped the cheese off his face. Just like I had the day before our first win here, eight years earlier. And every year after. Every year but last year. As I wiped it off, folding the napkin and dabbing a second time, it occurred to me that this week was the anniversary of my knowledge about Anne. The planet was just completing the orbit it had started that night at the pool, while Brah passed away from us into the darkness and Katie told me about what else had been hiding in the darkness of my life, the actions of those whose decisions I thought I could track, expect, and fathom. No matter what rituals I enacted, no matter how strongly I wished I could go back, the next year was starting. It was just going to keep on going and going and going. In midair I could read what the spin on a tennis ball would lead it to do. Watching the white seams spin, in a split second, I knew if the ball would jump, stand up, cut left or right. But I had no perspective on which way things were going in my life. Part of me hoped that it was all spinning away from what had been left behind. Part of me wanted it back.

Vincent Philippe and Darren Jessee were our first opponents. We knew when to cross. We knew when to play two back, when to poach. This was the gift of having played together for so long. You watch other doubles teams, and before each point it's like a conference. I knew a few players—singles specialists mostly—who had never played with the same partner in more than one tournament. But Kaz and I had a type of telepathy. At no moment did I ever find myself wondering what Kaz was going to do on court. I simply knew. Which worked well for us in that first match. Because we weren't speaking at all.

When I was at the net, I would crouch and give hand signals behind my back for which way to serve. But when we won a point, we didn't high-five. We didn't bump fists. During the third game of the first set, I overheard Philippe say he was going to serve into Kaz's body. I turned and pointed to my chest. Kaz then stepped around the ball when it came jumping at his torso and hit an inside-out forehand that froze Philippe in his shoes. We broke their serve that game, won the first set, and stayed on serve through the second. My first serve was dropping in around 55, 60 percent of the time, and when it did, the point was ours. Which was always the case. People hated playing me because they couldn't get into a rhythm. Some said it wasn't real tennis. That I had one trick: my serve. Manny had always said it was the only thing you had complete control of during a match, and though he hadn't been the one to think that up—it was every elementary coach's maxim—it was true. My serve wasn't a trick. It was a weapon. Kaz didn't serve his best during the match, but he was returning well, and that's really what got us up that break in the first set. The second went to a tiebreaker. Throughout it all, we didn't say a word. We didn't even yell *switch* or *mine*. We just showed up and went to work. And it went the way it always did at Forest Hills. We won.

After the match, Kaz stood shirtless in the locker room and held his diary open before him, like some sweaty minister sermonizing to a suspicious audience of one.

"You need to take an ice bath," he said. "Eat pesto penne by yourself. Warm up with Douglas Adams tomorrow. And call Anne."

Her name from his mouth hit me harder than I had expected.

"I'm not going to call her."

"No . . ." he looked closely at the page. "Yeah. You have to."

"Nope."

He held up the book like he had nothing to do with it. "It is what it is."

I shrugged and shook my head.

That night at the hotel, though, the phone seemed to grow larger and larger on the bedside table. I picked it up and set it down twice. Finally I picked it up and held it. It buzzed in my palm. I dialed.

"Hello?" Anne said. She sounded perfect. At ease. Healthy. "Hello? Helllooo? Anyone there?" I said nothing. She went into her *Airplane* shtick. "What's the vector, Victor? Roger, Roger. Over, Under." She listened for a few seconds, then hung up. The dead phone lay in my lap until the busy signal made me jump.

Douglas Adams was still on the tour. He was a shaggy blond lefty from Maryland with a chiseled chinstrap beard and a terrible serve who managed to hang around the 250s in singles without anyone understanding how.

"Once I played doubles with Jin-Ho Lee," Adams said, stretching his thighs at the net. It was the next morning. He pulled the heel of his left foot close to his lower back and grimaced. "I'd never even met him, just showed up on court, and when I asked him if he spoke English he waved his hand in the air like I'd farted."

"We both speak English."

"I know, I'm just saying it works without talking."

"That's what I'm saying."

"This isn't much of a conversation."

That afternoon, we lost the first set 4–6 to Tony Rodriguez and Phil Mackey. On the changeover, Kaz furiously flipped through the pages of his diary. He said, "You eat a banana?"

"I don't have a banana."

Kaz whispered, "Call a bathroom break and go get one. You need a banana."

"This is crazy," I said and just continued to the other side of the court.

The first point of the next game, Kaz hit a backhand return so deep it hit the back fence before bouncing. He hit an overhead into the net. He whiffed a forehand volley. He turned to me and opened his eyes wide, as if it were my fault. We lost the game at love. A subway was passing in the distance, NECK FACE painted in huge red letters across the first subway car. This could be my last match. Ever.

"Bathroom," I said to the chair umpire. "It's an emergency."

I knew there was one near the court, but I just walked towards the clubhouse, on the opposite side of the grounds, purposefully acting like I had no idea I was taking the longest route possible to a toilet. I stopped at the outdoor bar, where another one of the young men in a tuxedo stood serving no one.

"I need a banana," I said.

"No bananas."

I went into the dining room. A bathroom break officially gave you only three minutes. If they found me in a dining room we would be disqualified.

"I need a banana!" I said to a waiter with a shaved head and a very fine black moustache. A handful of elderly lunchers looked up from chicken salad on croissants.

"We only have banana smoothies, sir."

"What do you make them out of?"

The mustachioed waiter looked at me like I had just made a really good point. He stepped into the kitchen and—after what felt several minutes—emerged with a plastic cup filled with chopped pieces of frozen banana. I put as many of them into my mouth as would fit.

I bounded up the pathway. The banana was so hard I could just barely get my teeth into it. My head ached from the frozen core of my face. As I neared the court, I stuffed more banana into my mouth and tossed the cup into a trashcan. By the time I picked up my racquet, my head was splitting.

It was my serve.

One

I worried that I might have frozen part of my brain.

Two

In seventh-grade science class,

Three

I had read that popping a zit could send pus into your brain,

Four

resulting in brain damage.

Five

I still wonder if that could actually be true.

Six

It had established in me

Seven

a deep fear of brain injury through trivial action.

Eight

But

Nine

My brain must have been mostly thawed, because when I connected I served an ace out wide to Rodriguez's forehand. Then another down the line, past Mackey's forehand. Kaz pumped his fist and pointed at me with glee. It was only after I smiled back that I remembered I shouldn't.

After we won, Kaz said, "The floor!"

He didn't need to tell me. I knew I knew I knew. After our first second-round win in 2000, I slept on an air mattress with a leak. By 3:00 AM it had deflated enough that I had to get up and refill it. The next morning I awoke stiff and miserable, but we won that day, and so now the floor was mandatory. At the Days Inn I didn't have a faulty air mattress, so I just took the comforter off my bed, folded it in half lengthwise, and made a pallet on the floor. A diaper from some guest long ago lay wadded on the floor under the mattress. I stood and began to remake the bed, but then remembered the banana. I tossed the comforter back on the floor, in sight of the mystery diaper, and slept where I needed to sleep.

In the morning, I awoke sore and stiff and spent fifteen minutes stretching while a construction crew worked outside, sending large orange clouds of dust in dense swells against the window. I left a note for the maid that said PLEASE REMOVE DIAPER UNDER BED.

In the locker room I turned my back to Kaz and held my arms crossed against my chest, like Dracula sleeping. Kaz put his arms around me, and I smelled the odor of his two-match winning streak as he lifted my body into the air. In a sharp downward pump he cracked my spine. I grunted as my body elongated. Kaz then set me down and took his arms away. The soreness from the night before was gone. His trick, like always, had worked.

"Now do me," he said.

"You'll be alright," I said and opened the door.

"Hey. Seriously!"

"This is completely stupid."

"You keep saying that, but if this was stupid, you wouldn't be here."

He crossed his arms and turned. I looked at him there, expectant and trusting, then stepped back into the locker room, put my arms around him, and lifted him into the air. I bounced him harder than I ever had before, and as his body jerked in my arms, a low, guttural moan emerged from deep within his chest. I let go and he bent over, then held the position, his hands dangling just above his shoes, one scuffed and one perfect.

"Motherfucker," he whispered. "Oh Jesus."

"You OK?"

"No."

"I didn't mean to do that. Seriously. Hey, I'm serious."

"OK."

"Get up."

"Just leave me here for a second."

"I . . ."

He breathed short and shallowly as he tried to stand.

"Can I . . . ?" I stepped towards him.

"No! Just go."

On court, I drank a paper cup of ice water from the courtside cooler. It hurt my teeth, and I sucked them tight against my lips as I watched Hockney and May practice serves. Nine people total sat on a pair of aluminum bleachers beside us. Eight of them were old men, and one was a beautiful young blond with Hockney. The umpire said, "Everything OK?" and I nodded. But I didn't know. I had the sudden assurance that we were going to have to default, but then, as if in reproach to any doubt of routine, I saw Kaz slowly walking up the sidewalk, past the netless grass courts, and through the alleyway between tall chain-link.

He practiced three serves. On each, his toss looked fine, but at none did he swing. He still didn't speak to me, and I was almost tempted to ask him what he was going to do. Then he hit an underhand serve. Hockney and May didn't even notice. They thought he was returning the ball to the ball boy. But I knew. Kaz could barely move.

He served his first service game underhanded, and Hockney and May returned two first serves into the net. They sent one three feet long and floated another just wide. The balls were coming at them with so little pace they didn't even know what to do. We won the first set 6–2. By the start of the second, Kaz was loose and the cramp was gone. He swatted overheads like he always had and moved smoothly across the baseline. But still he served underhand. It was part of his new routine. I hoped we would never have to repeat it. By the end of the second set we had drawn one of the largest crowds I'd ever had at Forest Hills. They were there to see the spectacle. Old men laughed. Hockney's girlfriend had to leave. When Kaz served a drop-shot ace at 5–2, it was so ridiculous that I had to restrain myself from laughing. It

173

DOUBLES .....

was as if the way we played was inconsequential to the outcome. No matter what we did, as long as we did it together, as long as I wiped cheese off of his face, slept beside the diaper, ate at Teriyaki Boy, and listened to Anne recite her dead call monologue, we won.

23

JOG IN PLACE while listening to Snoop Dogg. Eat more penne pasta from Puttanesca on Ninth Avenue Sleep on the floor. Don't stretch at all when you wake. I did what I was supposed to do. I didn't question this magic anymore, even if the diaper still lay where it had. I hung the DO NOT DISTURB sign on the knob in hopes they would leave it there forever.

At the club, I bounced out of the locker room, past the empty grass courts on my right, past friends that were still in the draw warming up on the hard courts to my left. Our draw favored us. We had Yevgeny and Belanko, Polish teenagers who had been playing out of their minds but couldn't keep it up. I crossed into the narrow chain-link alley between courts and stepped onto Court 4, a lonely corner with a clear view of the elevated subway to the east. The Poles were already there, wearing tight, sleeveless T-shirts, stretching their calves with their feet propped against the fence. I took off my jacket and turned to the empty seats. But today the empty seats weren't empty. In two folding chairs set close against the chain-link sat Manny and Katie.

Manny's giant lips were stretched into an enormous grin. He wore cowboy boots and a white turtleneck sweater with an amber medallion on the outside. Katie had on an orange dress and white stockings. Her dark hair had been cut into heavy bangs, and she wore large sunglasses perched on her tiny nose. Her mouth moved ever so slightly, but it couldn't be called a smile. It was just movement. Every person who walked by looked at them as they passed. I could see people commenting to each other, pointing and staring. Manny called out, "Think you'd sneak this by us?"

I waved.

"Don't look so amazed," Manny said. "Think we could stay apart? We're like you and Kaz, man. We're bound to get back together."

I walked closer. I saw that Manny's medallion held a wasp enclosed in amber.

"Oh, we're not back together," I said. "It's just for this tournament."

"You're back together."

"We're barely talking."

"Kaz! You guys talking?"

I didn't know Kaz had even entered the court. I turned and there he was, stretching at the chair. He said, "We've barely said a word since Monday."

For some reason, everyone laughed. Even Katie. So I laughed too. I laughed about how I wasn't speaking to Kaz because I was mad at him for sleeping with my wife. I laughed because Katie seemed to have forgotten that I had asked her if she wanted me to do the monkey-style and then slept with her girlfriend. There was so much not to laugh about. But we laughed.

Play started, and I kept looking at Katie from the corner of my eye, silent and uncheering by the fence. I couldn't focus, couldn't even remember the score. But I didn't need to, because the chair umpire— the same sad soul who had officiated our duel—announced that we had won the first game. Then he told us that we won the second. And the third. And the fourth. And so on. By match point, Manny was yelling so much that the chair umpire said, "Mr. LaSalle, please respect the players."

"You remembered my name!" Manny said.

And I served another ace.

Immediately my thoughts went to the next match. It was the first thing to creep in beside Katie. Because we had one day off, and then it was Sunday. And the finals were on Sunday, and now we were in them. Without even checking the results I knew who we were going to face. Because the Simon brothers were here. And nobody beat them. We had played them six times in our career. We had won a total of nine games, no sets, no matches. But we didn't lose at Forest Hills. Something was going to give.

While packing my bag in silence, I tried to envision a way past those wankers, but I was interrupted when Manny called out, "Slow!"

I turned. He stood by the fence texting.

"Slow, seriously. I just gotta say, man. Slow." He beckoned me over without raising his eyes. "Before you go. Slow, the photos." He then closed the phone and finally looked up. "I mean."

I zipped my racquets into the bag and said, "Photos?"

"The *photos*."

I looked at Katie for help.

She said, "One of my galleries took Anne's photos."

"Which ones?"

"The ones you took."

I'd left the Polaroids in that French Open bag when I walked out of University Hospital. Some days I imagined they were pinned to her wall. Other times I felt sure she had thrown them away. She tossed items easily—her yearbooks, stuffed animals from her childhood, greeting cards immediately after she read them. But the photos were artifacts of our private worlds of pain, extrapolated and spread over months. It was nice to think that they had mattered to anyone.

"They're amazing," Katie said. "I'll show you."

24

KATIE AND I got out of the cab beneath an overpass on the corner of Twenty-third and Tenth. A storefront beside me was shut with a metal curtain padlocked to the curb. Three young Asian women in short dresses and bright leggings passed by, speaking loudly about construction on the west side. I felt conspicuous in my pants. They were the kind that zipped off into shorts. Katie paid the fare while I waited beside a full-length window displaying a large variety of bonsai trees circling a small village made out of Legos and populated with live mice.

"That's Tartaglia," she said as we passed.

Another window featured paintings of deer walking through empty cityscapes. The divide in our lives suddenly seemed more vast than I had ever imagined. We passed a large sculpture of red metal I-beams filling a white room under a group of used Big Gulps glued to the walls. Then I came upon another large white industrial space filled with Polaroids. I didn't have to count how many photos were in there. I knew: 542. I had taken almost all of them.

People stood inside, staring silently, taking in the profile of Anne against our purple hallway, a shade chosen because we had found three extra gallons of the paint in our attic when we moved in, her stomach bulging inch by inch. For 187 photos of her in profile, there was a small remote in her left hand, wire extending from it towards the camera. I walked counterclockwise through the large space, watching her stomach close in on the closet doorknob. In photo 124, she looked at the camera, laughing.

"What's she laughing at?" Katie said.

"I'd just stepped into the hallway," I said. I hadn't been wearing anything but sunglasses. It was one of my oldest gags. I didn't tell her about that, though. I didn't want to talk. I wanted to look.

Anne held the hem of her shirt to her chest, baring the expanding flesh of her belly. For weeks her hip bones continued to jut out further than her stomach. Then she filled with the rounding life.

After number 187, a small sign made out of vinyl lettering read:

ON APRIL 25, 2006, ANNE SMITH AND HER HUSBAND WERE INVOLVED IN AN AUTOMOBILE ACCIDENT NEAR THEIR HOME IN NORTH CAROLINA. THE IMPACT LEFT ANNE IN A COMA. FOR THE NEXT 236 DAYS, HER HUSBAND CONTINUED TO PHOTOGRAPH HER. IT IS HIS HANDWRITING YOU SEE ON THE BOTTOM OF PHOTOS 192–542.

Above the vinyl lettering was a Polaroid of me, one of the series Anne had taken of me leaning over my front leg, bouncing a tennis ball. Counting. On the bottom was written SLOW COUNTING, INDIANAPOLIS, RCA, 3.7.04. MY HUSBAND = BIG WEIRDO! I LOVE HIM.

Then Anne lay in bed, her face swollen into a dried apricot crusted with blood. Over the space of a few yards of wall, the swelling disappeared and was replaced by withering, shrinking, the slow recession of her lips. Then for dozens of photos, nothing changed except for the light. Finally, at the end of the line, there was one photo that stood out like an exclamation point. It was labeled THE FIRST DAY AWAKE, and in it Anne looked directly at the camera, her spooky eyes swollen from crying. It was shocking, even there, to see her come back to life.

"Excuse me," a young woman said, laying her hand on my arm.

I turned. The hand belonged to one of the Asian women who had passed me on the sidewalk. She pointed to the photo of me. I nodded.

She said. "This." She held out her small round hand. "Is so beautiful."

"OK."

"Where is she?"

"I don't know."

"You don't know?"

"I don't know," I said. I whispered, "She's a terrible person."

The woman stepped away in shock. I turned back to the photos, my face on fire. When I next moved she was gone.

At the end of the room I found more vinyl wall text. It read ON FRIDAY, JUNE 12, AT 3PM, SMITH WILL GIVE A GALLERY TALK AND SIGN COPIES OF *ANNE SMITH*, THE 230-PAGE FULL-COLOR CATALOGUE.

Behind the information desk sat a young man with a shaved head who wore a khaki suit two sizes too small. He looked at me as I approached like I was going to ask him for spare change.

"So that's my wife," I said. "And I was wondering if I could leave a note for her that you could give to her tomorrow?"

"Who?"

"Anne Smith."

"You'd have to email the gallery."

"She's my wife."

"Anne Smith?"

"Yes," I said. I walked to the photo of me on the wall and pointed at it.

"Don't touch the artwork."

"That's me. I *took* these."

The suit walked around the front of the desk, and a group of young men with rattails stopped to watch. He leaned closer to the photo, then looked at me.

"Weird," he said. "But you're really going to have to email the gallery."

"Just. Here." I walked to the desk, picked up a postcard with a photo of Anne sleeping on the front, lifted a pen from beside the computer keyboard, and I wrote COME TO KATIE'S TOMORROW FOR CHARADES. 7PM. slow. "Here." I handed him the postcard. "See? It's perfectly normal. Just put it right there, beside your keyboard. When she comes in give it to her."

"I can't promise anything unless you email the gallery."

"Hunter," Katie said. The man in the suit looked at her like she owned him. "Give her the note."

At the sight of Katie, he vigorously nodded yes, of course he would give her the note.

We waited outside for a cab.

"Thanks for pulling rank," I said.

"What'd it say?"

"To come to your place for charades."

"We're doing that again?"

"Can't stop now."

I held my hand high above our heads, and a cab finally slowed on its path down Ninth. We would be taking separate cars in different directions, so this was it for a while. As it came to a stop I said, "I want to apologize about Paige."

"You did me a favor."

The driver—a man with a turban and a very large beard—bent down in the seat to see what the holdup was.

"Manny is completely insane. I know. But I love him."

"What's wrong with us?" I said.

"What do you mean?"

"All of us. Why do we all do this stupid shit?"

The cab honked.

"Go on," I said.

The cabbie rolled the window down and yelled, "You getting in?"

But Katie didn't move. She just waved the cab away with her hand and said, "I want to show you something."

I followed her west on Twenty-third, past the same galleries, the Big Gulps and the mice and Anne. We crossed Tenth, occupied with odd car dealerships and apartment buildings, and emerged on the west side north of Chelsea Piers. Still I followed, silent. Katie walked a path that ran down to the river past a large area of excavated earth behind a chain-link fence, rocks hewn up from the ground and piled in mounds that rose above us, the holes from which they emerged kept far from view, deep and hidden. It was a city riverwalk under construction, almost deserted. A metal pier, probably unused for sixty years, a hundred maybe, more even, stretched into the Hudson, its skeleton warped and collapsed into a series of arthritic architectural fingers crossed and reaching out of the water. And through that tangle of moldering metal shone the setting sun, orange and oblong and all ours, of all things in this city. The path led along an area of rocks made into a short bank. The area adjacent to the pier was strangely free of debris. The bank was long and shallow, and the Hudson washed simple and clean around the base of a giant black corroded steel girder, swirling into a tiny eddy past the metal, under the shadow of the pier. Katie stepped off the path and approached the metal, and I stood on the path and watched. She stopped just short of the water. The breeze off the river was colder than it had been only blocks away, and she held her arms around her small torso. Her green blouse whipped around her slender waist, flashing tan flesh beneath. I thought of Anne on the pontoon, when she had held herself against the cold that first afternoon we'd met. I waited for a sign, a movement, but nothing came. Silent and careful, I approached and stopped beside Katie.

She said, "I come here all the time."

"It's beautiful," I said, nervous I'd admitted some aesthetic blunder.

She nodded. "I always want to get in."

"Then get in."

"That's the Hudson."

"So what?"

She looked at me like she'd never seen me before. It thrilled me that I had surprised her.

"Get in," I said again.

"Really?"

"I don't know. Why not?"

"Because I might drown like the last time we got near water."

"You didn't drown, though. Remember? I saved you."

She stepped out of her shoes and flinched when she stepped into the water, but kept going until it lapped up her ankles, then deeper, slowly letting it rise, until she was waist-deep. Then she turned and said what I guess I knew she was going to say. "Come on."

Only blocks away, Hunter in his miniature suit had my post-card, cabs flew by restaurants, construction carried on. Here there was sunset, water, and Katie. It was a year ago that I had joined her in underwear in water, a year to the day probably, when I had jumped into the pool in the dark and Katie had told me about Anne. I unzipped my pants so that they turned into shorts, took off my sweatshirt and hat, and stepped into the Hudson. Katie let herself fall back into the water, and I did the same. The water was surprisingly clean. My eyes rose to the pinking sky. We let the river wash us into the shadow of the crumbling pier, where the ground opened up, a sudden deep ravine that swept our feet out from under us. Panic rushed through me for an instant, but we did not wash downstream. We floated softly and easily into the eddy and found ourselves caught in an urban whirlpool, the sky changing pastels through the metal crosses and curves above. We circled each other, not touching, not speaking, just orbiting the same center, carried on that same steady current, letting it carry us to the same spot again and again and again.

25

ONE OF MANNY'S cowboy boots stood in the middle of Katie's living room as if it had been crossing the room on its own and just stopped there to look for something. The sports section was spread open on the coffee table, dangling off the edge and on to the carpet. I heard Kaz and Manny laughing from the small balcony above. When I closed the door behind me they stopped. I walked upstairs, under the African masks, past the fireplace that still burned and still gave off no heat. Kaz looked at me like I had just told him to use inside voices. Manny held up his fist black-pride-style. On the coffee table lay pencils, torn paper, a bowl, a cowboy hat, a beer bottle, and some Gatorade. A stopwatch hung around Manny's neck.

"Let's wang chung," Manny said.

"We gotta wait," I said.

"Katie! Get me a beer?" he called over the balcony.

"I'm serious."

He started dividing the paper into groups.

"*Wait.*"

"What for?"

"Anne."

Kaz looked up.

"She in town?"

I nodded.

"What for?"

"Thing at the gallery," Manny said.

"I left her a note."

"A note?"

"What gallery?" Kaz said.

"A note?"

"We have to do it the same," I said.

"She didn't always play," Kaz said. "We're *doing* it the same."

"I'm not talking about charades."

The only thing that moved in the room was the silent, cold fire.

Kaz looked at his filthy fingernails.

I said it again. "We have to do it the same."

"I don't get it," Manny said.

"You're gonna have to do it again."

Kaz wouldn't look up.

"What's he have to do?" Manny said.

"He knows."

"He doesn't look like it."

For a second I worried that Manny was right, that Kaz didn't know what I meant. But then he finally looked up at me through those dark, thin eyebrows, and it was clear that he knew he had to do it too.

"What's he have to do? What?" Manny said.

"He's got to sleep with Anne."

The room fell silent.

I had not seen Anne since she had gotten out of her hospital bed, had not seen her walk since she had drifted mad across the moss more than a year ago and gotten into the Dart. I settled into a hard-backed wooden chair and waited for her to arrive. When she did, it was in a pale green vintage dress and yellow high heels and without most of her hair. It had been cut into a short red bowl cut, straight and severe and boyish. She looked from me to Manny to Kaz, the men of her life, and Manny said, "OK. It's a movie . . . One syllable . . . *Ghost*."

"My back hurts," she said and sat on the floor. She leaned against an empty plush seat like she'd been here dozens of times.

We looked around the room, each waiting for the other. Kaz's eyes darted from Anne to Manny to me and back. Together we had pushed each other to tears, driven ourselves to carve names into our shoulders and thrill each other by promising monkey-style. Together we had pursued our dreams until they were our currency, until we traded on what we thought was their limitless value. But there was a limit, and we had reached it, had lived that saturation point for years. There was no real striving anymore, just this repetition of success with diminishing returns. One year off, though, just one cycle, made me want it all again more than ever. Here were the people I lived my life with. Here were the people who had seen me fail and conquer over decades. They made me feel old, like those shoppers in Forest Hills. Old and strong and confident and glad that their youth was gone. These were the loves of my life.

"We gonna wang chung?" Manny said.

Anne pursed her lips a little and ran a hand through her bowl cut. I saw the bottom of a tattoo peek out from her sleeve. It hadn't been there before.

"I know you need me here to complete whatever spell you're casting," she said.

We listened to the silence, full and swelling.

"OK then," Manny finally said. "This is a little game I like to call charades."

Manny, me, and Katie. Kaz and Anne. The teams were always the same. With Manny's input, our scraps filled with the names of Westerns. Kaz and Anne were settled into the love seat. Nervous and awkward, they silently wrote clues onto strips of paper and dropped them into a yellow plastic mixing bowl.

"I don't think they know what *Hondo* is," Katie whispered.

"Yeah they do," Manny said.

"*A Fist Full of Dollars?*"

"Everybody knows that."

He wrote the names of more and more Westerns onto the scraps and tossed them into one of his cowboy hats. He was the only confident one in the room. Before he was done, I wrote one clue of my own. It said *Big*. It was the first movie Anne and I had ever seen together. In the years since, no movie was good enough for Anne. Watching with her, she either sighed at bad scenes or simply fell asleep. *Big*, though—which we had rented and watched on my thirteen-inch television in my old apartment with the lights out during a summer thunderstorm, the screen doors to the porch open, water spraying in on us from time to time—she had loved. I dropped the word into the bowl, and as soon as it was handed to Kaz, I said, "Wait. I want to change one."

"Too late," Anne said and took the bowl greedily.

I drew first. The piece of paper said CAROLINA FRIENDS SCHOOL.

"This isn't even a category," I said.

"Go on," Manny said. "You got this one."

I sighed. I held up a peace sign. I opened a book. I tried to indicate I was wearing a large straw hat and had a large beard, like the Quaker from the oats.

"Grizzly Adams!" Manny yelled.

"What are you doing?" Katie said. "What's he doing?"

I took off my shoes. I sat cross-legged and raised my hand like I wanted to be called upon. Kaz said, "Time."

"Friends School," I said.

"*Friends* School Friends School?" Katie said.

"Yeah. Friends School."

"That's nothing," Manny said.

"I know."

"What do you mean it's nothing?" Anne said.

"It's not a real clue."

"He just did it, didn't he?"

Manny shook his head in disgust. "Barely."

Anne fished around the cowboy hat.

Katie whispered, "That really shouldn't count. It really shouldn't."

"I know," Manny said. They clutched hands.

Anne lifted a clue, looked at it with disgust, then cranked an invisible camera.

"Movie!" Kaz yelled.

Anne stopped cranking. "I don't even know what this is."

"At least it's a category," I said.

"Get phonetic," Manny said.

"Give her another one," Katie said, annoyed.

"That's not how it works."

"*The Magnificent Seven*?" Anne said.

"Oh my God," Manny said.

"What is it?"

"Just hold up seven fingers and do something magnificent."

"This is bullshit," she said and drew again.

"Wait!"

But she was already cranking another camera, rolling her eyes. The tattoo crept out from her arm again, and I saw that it was a small bird in flight.

"Movie," Kaz said, glad to latch on to something. "Two words. First word . . . small word. OK. A? The? The!" He followed as she tapped on her forearm. "Second word. OK. Two syllables . . ."

She placed a hand on her forehead as if she were shielding the sun from her eyes and then looked across the room, squinting.

"Look, looking. The Look," Kaz said. "The Squint. The Confusion."

Anne began to get frantic. She bent and looked under the love seat, then around its back. It was amazing to see her so active.

"Lost. Looking. Search. Search? Search!"

Anne waved yes! Like she was trying to waft the smell of the answer into her nose.

"The Search! The Search! The Search! What? The Searcher! The Search! The Searching! The Search! Searching! What? The Searcher!"

She nodded towards Manny, as if Kaz had gotten it. Manny only laughed. The word was becoming meaningless the more Kaz repeated it.

"Searcher. Search. Search. Searching. Searcher . . ."

Manny could barely hold himself together, laughing so hard that he could no longer make noise, just silently gulp air.

"Time," he finally gasped. "Time!"

"What was it?" Kaz said.

"Sear*chers*," Manny said.

"I said that."

"He said that."

"Not the plural," Katie said.

"Oh my God," Kaz said, falling hard into the love seat beside Anne.

"I don't even know what it is," Anne said.

"*The Searchers*?" Manny said.

"Yes."

"The best movie ever."

"We still get it, though," said Anne.

"He didn't get it," Katie said. "No way."

Anne held her arms into the air.

"I can't believe I came here for this," she said, then picked up the hat full of clues. She pulled one out and read it. "*Hang 'Em High*?" She tossed it over her shoulder. "*Rancho Notorious*?" Over her shoulder. "*Hondo . . . Hondo*? That's not even a word. *Hondo*? These are bullshit." She dumped the hat on the ground. Small pieces of paper flew everywhere.

"Stop!" Manny said, grabbing clues by the fistful. Everyone was laughing now, even Anne. She settled back in the love seat beside Kaz, and I was overwhelmed with jealousy. I longed for her. I fantasized about my own wife. As everyone laughed, I forced myself to laugh along with them.

Manny stood. He wound the air beside his ear.

"Movie!" we shouted.

He ran in exaggerated slow motion while grinning at us, his huge lips stretched with joy across his angular face. He never broke the clues down into words or syllables. He just tried to convey the essence. His arms extended and retracted at a glacial pace while each knee slowly rose almost to his chest. At times he would stop to warm his hands by an imaginary fire.

Katie yelled, *"The Running Man! Rocky! She's Got Legs! Catch Me if You Can! The Fugitive!"*

I just let her go on. Anne and Kaz laughed and whispered. Like me, they knew it was *Chariots of Fire*. I just tried to look confused.

"Cool Runnings! Um um um *The Gods Must Be Crazy! Ben-Hur!"*

Manny's grin faded as he continued to run.

"Time!" Kaz said.

Manny's limbs ground to a halt.

"Ben-Hur?" he said.

"What was it?" I said.

"Ben-Hur?"

"What?" Katie said. "What was it?"

"What part of me said *Ben-Hur?"*

"What was it?"

"Ben fucking Hur? *Chariots of Fire!"*

"Agh!" I said.

I put my hands on my face in disgust. Through my fingers I saw Anne watching. I wondered if she was detecting the fake. But then

Kaz stood and wound the air, and she shifted her attention. Another movie. They were all movies. He pulled invisible fistfuls of dollars from his pockets while my wife squealed in pleasure. Manny grew increasingly furious as we lost and lost again. I held my tongue with each movie I knew. Everyone laughed more and more. I knew we had to lose for this equation to work. They needed the win to celebrate.

I said, "I need to get back."

"There's more clues," Manny said.

"Ah." I waved my hand in the air. "You guys finish without me."

Anne and Kaz waved simultaneously.

I walked downstairs and heard Kaz yell, "Movie! One word! One syllable!"

I looked up at the landing. Anne stood with her back to me. She put her hands around her stomach, indicating that it was huge.

"Fat!"

She held her hands high above her head.

"Tall!"

She shook her head, crouched down, then spun. As she spun she grew taller with each turn, as if she were in a magical whirlwind.

"Spin!"

When she reached her full height, she held her hands high above her head and finished her turn. When she stopped, she was facing me. I looked up at her, stretching long towards the ceiling, a sliver of a human who had once been mine. Her eyes lowered. It was the woman whom I had aspired to fit, the one I had almost killed. She had stood with her arms above her head just like that at the edge of the pontoon. From the balcony she looked into me, and it felt like she was diving into my face. It was the first private moment we'd had since the hospital. She looked alive and tall and thin and like a different person with her hair and tattoo, now completely visible on the side of her shoulder. She rose in one last push, lifting onto her tiptoes, and Kaz yelled, "Big!"

26

I PLACED THE containers of Go-Gurt on the bench beside me and took the packet of Ex-Lax from my sweatshirt pocket. I stuck my finger into the Go-Gurt on the right. I licked it off. Blueberry. I stuck my finger into the one on the left. I licked it. Raspberry. I ate one spoonful of raspberry, one blueberry. Then I took an Ex-Lax. I jogged in place while humming "Born to Run," then bounced away from the bench, slowly crossing the locker room as I felt my system begin to behave. I jogged directly to the toilet, dropped my pants, and sat. My body obeyed like a machine. I showered for a second time. I finished the blueberry Go-Gurt. I drank two orange Gatorades then finished the raspberry Go-Gurt. I didn't need Kaz here to tell me any of this. I had done it enough to know.

The locker room was always empty on Sunday. Everyone else had already lost and flown to Paris. I always beat Kaz to the court for the final. I never knew why he was late in the past. This year I knew.

I dressed and left before he arrived. When I emerged from the locker room, the Simon brothers stood on the landing. Sam, the one who wore a tight beaded choker necklace, said, "Slow. You gonna count all day? I'm just giving you a hard time. When you going to France?"

We would only qualify for the French Open if we won today. "Tomorrow, I guess."

"Gonna say we should ride together."

Sandy, the lefty, waved while talking on his cell phone. He said, "I don't know if they serve chicken or not. I don't know. I don't know how else to say it. They might. They might not."

"I gotta," I said, pointing towards the courts. I couldn't stand to hear Sandy talk about chicken for another second.

"Oh yeah," Sam said, like he had forgotten there was a match to be played. "I'll see you out there in a bit."

But I didn't go to the courts. I left the gates and headed into the streets of Forest Hills, running as hard as I could. I passed under the low-hanging branches, heavy with ephemeral blossoms. A woman got out of a Lincoln Town Car with a young girl carrying a large stuffed panda. The father, in flip-flops and khaki shorts, took bags from the trunk. I ran by them. Another couple pushed a baby carriage towards me. I had passed from the elderly into the family district. I kept running. I passed through a small area beneath an overpass lined with Mexican bakeries and a storefront filled with pastel formal dresses. Back into affluence, past brownstone stairs leading older couples home from church. The first year I had run this route I made eye contact with everyone I passed in hopes someone would recognize me. But these people didn't even know that the West Side Tennis Club existed. And if they did, they didn't care. I crossed through the bustling plaza near the subway stop and entered the tunnel of vegetation leading back to the club. I turned left onto the block where the club was. A cab was stopped at the curb. I stopped in the shade of a gingko tree. Kaz stepped out of the cab, slowly setting his tennis bag on the sidewalk before searching his sweatshirt for his wallet. After he paid, he ambled slowly towards the clubhouse, stepping carefully over every crack.

Court 1 was packed with the usual geriatric set. I wondered what it was like to watch men perform feats no longer possible for you. But as I saw the tanned faces on those old men, I suddenly had the feeling that these captains of industry all still thought they could do what I did. They didn't look like they were dying. They all looked confident and tan and happy.

Manny and Katie were already seated courtside. They started to cheer when I stepped on court. "Slow it down," Manny yelled. "Slow it down, ladies and gentleman."

He wore a brown polyester suit that looked like it had come from the Mexican wedding store under the subway. His amber medallion glimmered atop a white cowboy shirt. Katie wore a lime green dress and a wide white hat. I worried about the people who had to sit behind them.

Kaz said nothing as he walked to the chair. He looked more drawn than normal, but I smelled him as he passed, and he smelled terrible, so that was a good sign. We did not speak. We hit practice serves side by side. We traded groundstrokes with the Simons. We stood at the net and hit volleys, then lifted our eyes to the sun, a blurry, shifting orb lingering in my vision as I snatched overheads out of the air.

Play began with Sam Simon serving. He didn't serve as fast as I did, but he placed them well. They won the game. Which was fine. We didn't have many looks. I hit two aces in the next game, and we chalked up our tenth game ever against them. By the time we switched sides, my jitters were gone.

On Kaz's serve, he tossed the first ball too far in front and dumped it into the net. His second serve floated long. It often took Kaz a few minutes to ease into a match. At the net I switched sides and leaned low to give him clearance. The Simon brothers bounced from side to side simultaneously. A ball flew over my shoulder and landed three feet long. I heard Kaz bounce another three times behind me as I stood and reset. The Simon brothers began to bounce again. Sam was so close to the net that I could hear the beads on his necklace click with each hop. My shadow stretched just over the net, a squat, dark mass that moved with me as I swayed from side to side. The angle of the shadow meant the sun was behind us. Kaz could see the ball as well as he was going to, but it didn't matter. His next serve hit almost the same spot as its errant predecessor. A murmur rose. A double double fault.

Kaz took his time moving to the deuce court, then just stood there, leaning forward on his one stiff leg, perched above that scuffed shoe. He had always mocked me for my counting, but I now wondered if he wasn't trying it for himself. He should have been. I watched him from the corner of my eye. When he bounced the ball it hit the toe of his shoe and rolled into the middle of the court. A hesitant and beautiful ball girl who couldn't have been more than fourteen rushed after it.

I heard one of the old men courtside say, "This puppy's got a problem."

His first serve went long. My shadow was motionless. I heard Kaz start to bounce the other ball behind me, and the sudden thought that he had not slept with my wife filled me with a rush of panic. Without this win, I would have enough points to go back into the satellite circuit, but at age thirty-one that seemed like the prospect of learning to walk all over again. I didn't know how to face a return to the office. I could only bear that job knowing it was temporary. I needed this match. I needed him to complete whatever sequence he had started. The ball then soared past my head, crossed the net, and dropped in the middle of the box, and Sandy drilled it at my face. I knifed it cross-court, and it skidded off the line. One point and my panic was gone. Kaz had done what he needed to do.

For the first time since we had first played them in juniors at age thirteen, we now had a match point on the Simons. I crouched at the T of the service boxes. This was a long, slow process that drove Kaz crazy, but which I had to take my time completing because of my knees and back, both of which were almost always so tight that if I knelt any faster, I felt like one or the other might snap. I lowered myself slowly, and then, once I was an inch or so above the court, let myself drop. Once a doubles player puts himself on the T, his partner can serve over him, but the opposing team doesn't know where he is going to go. I held my hand behind my back and jerked my thumb to the left. Kaz's first serve landed two feet wide. I had already started to move. I reset, forcing Kaz to wait out the process of dropping once again. During the whole laborious process the Simons bounced from side to side like two eager puppies. I finally dropped to the surface again, then motioned towards the same spot as before.

Kaz served another safe second serve, and I rose. Sam laid into it like a T-ball, returning it crosscourt so that it skidded into the empty space behind me. Kaz lunged with his backhand, just catching the ball on the frame. It rose high into the sky. The Simons were on the side of court facing the sun, and as Sam raised his racquet and backstepped into position, I hoped that the sun might blind him enough the cause him to shank it. It did not. He was two inches taller than his brother, and fifteen pounds heavier, and he slammed the ball out of the air with about twice as much speed as Kaz's serve had had.

The ball came at my waist. I raised my racquet with the head pointed at my toes, as if pulling it out of some morass. The strings met the ball just above the handle, just enough to propel it forward. It dinked over the net, and I almost screamed in joy. Match point on the Simon brothers was a once in a lifetime chance. But then of course, in the matter of time it took for Sam to reach the ball, I knew that was the exact thing I should not be thinking of. That that was the kind of thought that would make me play safe, tentative, and tight, and that I should be thinking about nothing, just feeling and reacting.

Very few people consistently lobbed over me. My height created problems that only two or three other guys on the tour could generate.

But the Simons—what can I say? They lobbed with the best of them. And I knew when I saw the ball rise from Sam's racquet that it would be a perfect lob. Kaz got to it, though, and flicked it crosscourt. But it caught the tape.

There are dozens of times a match that the ball hits the net cord. Some are service lets; others cut the ball off and drop it. Very few rise back into the air—in essence a coin toss—the direction almost always unclear. Even less frequently does this happen on a match point. The ball hung in the air for what seemed an eternity, and once again I questioned whether Kaz had completed his task. Then it fell onto the other side of the court. Sandy Simon lunged forward and got to the ball only after its second small bounce.

I dropped my racquet and looked up at the E train passing to the east. Manny screamed a terrifying guttural whoop, then gave a high five to an elderly woman in a wheelchair. Kaz fell to his knees and kissed the clay. When he looked back up, the green Forest Hills clay was caked to his lips. NECK FACE was passing again in the distance, and I wondered if it was the very same train I had seen before or if it was simply another tag on another car. It didn't matter if it was the original or the duplicate, though. What mattered was that the Simon brothers were waiting to shake our hands at the net, and I suddenly had a fondness for them. I was nostalgic for the moment as I was in it. Sandy shook my hand and put his other arm around me, pulling me into a brief embrace. I almost started to cry. Kaz took the last ball from his pocket and tossed it into the stands. Three old men stood from their folding chairs and held their arms into the air, pushing and straining for it as it fell.

part

3

27

MANNY SAT ON my floor, his freakish limbs snaking across the bare wooden floorboards. Sunlight lit dust floating through the room. I'd let Anne have the couch, the television, the wooden bench, the chair that had been my parents', the floor lamp shaped like an arrow, and the old wooden chest that we used as a coffee table. I had yet to replace anything. I was traveling so much that most of the time it didn't matter what was here anyway. I sat on the floor opposite Manny, my own long limbs stretched across the scratched hardwood. We bounced a tennis ball back and forth, avoiding the small pile of paper on the floor between our legs. One pink tab extended from its edges.

Outside, the grille of Manny's Fiat was bare. The horns were gone. He was wearing Stan Smiths, not cowboy boots. His season of Westerns had ended. After Kaz and I had won Forest Hills, I started to win with other players. Owen Philip and I made it to the second week at the U.S. Open. Kaz was there too, his luck also improving with others. But none of our results were as good as they had been when we were together. Kaz lost in the second round, and when Owen and I played Brown and Baldwin in the quarters, Katie came back to North Carolina with me and she and Manny remarried with the magistrate in the Chapel Hill police station, a building that looked like a UFO from 1950 that had landed in a hillside. Manny had been traveling with me since, hitting, coaching, stringing more racquets. We had been at it for three months.

Now we were off for a week because we hadn't made the cut for Montreal. The results had been mediocre, enthralling, and tempting. But we had been offered security in the least likely of places: state jobs playing tennis. After the fall semester, Coach Jester was retiring at UNC. They asked me to take his spot, and Manny to assist. We couldn't turn it down. This month was my last on tour, no matter what the result. Because two more years of wins might still result in no long-term job at all, no money, and no idea of what to do. I had to take what I had when I could.

"She's going to have to sign them," Manny said. "I know how this goes."

"I'd rather just mail them."

"You gotta do it in person."

"I'll do it."

"I'm serious."

"I don't even know where she lives."

"I know where she lives." He shrugged. "What? I had to drop off her photos."

I threw the ball back to him, and he let it bounce right past.

"Come on," he said and pushed himself up slowly and awkwardly, like a horse rising from a nap. The ball rolled down the hallway and into the empty guest room.

"Why didn't you tell me?"

"You didn't need to know."

He picked up the papers, opened the door, and stepped onto the porch. I followed, pulled along again. So many times. Out of bed. To practice. To Forest Hills. Off a chain-link fence. To duel. Now, to divorce. I wondered if, without Manny, I would have ever done anything.

We stepped into the front yard, damp from a rain shower that morning. It was September, and birds were singing in the two over-grown azaleas. Scattered leaves from the high oaks above had fallen

204

into a thin orange sheet onto the moss below. The bushes were taller than Manny. Anne had made me trim them three years earlier, but they had come back larger than ever, taller even than our small dogwood. As Manny passed one of the giant things, he reached over and shook it. More oak leaves tumbled out of it, and water fell off the web of branches in a small suburban rush. Two cardinals, a loud red male and a camouflaged brown female, screamed as they lifted to a limb above. One rabbit fled from beneath, scurrying past Manny's feet, leaping over the drainage ditch beside the road and disappearing into the woods on the opposite side of the street. Manny shook off his arm and started the Fiat.

Past the tennis court we turned onto the gravel road that ended at the tail end of Glen Lennox, an old series of duplex cottages built in the '40s and now filled mostly with graduate students and retired professors. We passed eight or ten of the little buildings, then turned into a small cul-de-sac. We weren't even a half mile from my house.

"No," I said.

Manny had always been like this: part coach, part psychiatrist, deciding what I did and didn't need to know. The low brick bungalow was nondescript. It had a well-kept lawn and no exterior decoration.

"She's not home," I said.

"She's home."

He turned off the ignition. I took the papers and started up the thin concrete path. The stalks of mowed weeds were thick in the cracks. I carefully avoided stepping on each of them. Before I got even halfway, Anne opened the storm door.

I looked down. I was on a crack. I looked back up. Anne stood on the threshold in a blue and white dress, one of her vintage ones, stitched in a pattern of fleur-de-lis. Her hair was still short, and now there were more tattoos: A flock of small black sparrows flew from the base of her thumb up the flesh of her forearm, scattering as they ascended. I didn't know how she spent her days anymore, what mysteries the rest of her body hid.

"Hi," she said, and motioned me inside. I looked back at Manny. He was leaning against his Fiat and waving to a baby in a stroller that cried as it neared him.

The living room was our old living room. The same furniture was arranged the same way. The window was in the same spot and faced the same direction. I sat in my old chair, the one my father had refinished when he had first married my mother. Anne sat where she always did, at the edge of the couch facing me, her good ear closest. I held up the divorce papers.

"Here," she said and leaned forward. She took them from my hand, laid them on the coffee table, flipped to the page with the tab on it, and lifted a pen from the top of a half-empty crossword.

"You don't have to do it right now."

She put the pen to paper and signed, then set it back atop the crossword. "You just play . . . Thailand?"

"Uh. Casablanca," I said, stunned.

"With who?"

"Jordan."

"You gonna keep playing with him?"

I shrugged.

"You alright?"

I shrugged.

She said, "You OK with this?"

She pointed at the papers. I stuck out my bottom lip. Her camera was on the table beside her.

"Pick that up," I said.

I felt a thrill unvisited by my system in months as she pushed the viewfinder against one spooky blue eye.

"The wreck," I said. "It was my fault."

The flash exploded. Anne calmly placed the dark photo on the table, then lifted the pen—the one that had just ended our marriage—and wrote THE WRECK, IT WAS MY FAULT onto the white space at the bottom.

"How?" she said, calm and detached, like a detective investigating our lives.

"The brakes."

"What part?"

"The footplate. It fell off."

"I remember you looking around for something."

"Yeah. That's what it was."

The room dimmed as a cloud passed in front of the sun. Anne looked at me and nodded. My deepest secret and she nodded, as if she had already known. I pointed at the camera. She put the camera back to her eye, more slowly than before.

I said, "And I know you and Kaz slept together again this year, after charades." No flash. She lowered the camera.

"I know," I said.

She looked around the room like she might find someone else to ask.

"He tell you that?" Anne said.

"He didn't have to. I made him promise me."

I opened my right hand in the air, palm to the ceiling, the logic of our routine obvious. She looked at me through the dust, lit here the same as it was in our house—my house—illuminated by the now horizontal sunbeams cutting through the room and landing on the wall in a sharp orange stencil of the window.

"Kaz left ten minutes after you did."

Anne might hide a secret for years, but once she spoke, she almost never lied. I could tell this was the truth.

"Come here," she said.

I didn't move.

"Come here," she said and patted the cushion beside her.

I walked across the floor. She grabbed the pocket of my jeans and pulled me down. If they hadn't done it all, exactly the same, that meant that there was credit beyond bananas and deflated mattresses, that my faith in our voodoo had been nonsense. That we had won not because I had wiped cream cheese off Kaz's face at the right time and place, but we had won because we had won. She put her hand on my knee. I had a brief taste of what it was like to be with someone you were not married to. I buried my face into her neck and held it there. She smelled like suntan lotion. I put my hands under her shirt and felt the sides of her stomach. I avoided touching the scar in the middle. We kissed sloppy and wet. We were rushing, not because Manny was outside, but because it felt like this was something that could stop, and I didn't want to give it the chance.

There were tattoos everywhere, those little birds I had seen on her wrist multiplied across her bare flesh. The scar on her stomach was a smooth flat line. She had smaller scars on her back, holes filled in with flesh up and down her spine. Residue of the accident. I had never seen them. I felt them as my fingers inched along her skin. She climbed on top of me, and then we fell onto the floor. I rolled on top of her and said, "You alright?" and she said, "What?" Her eyes were closed. She couldn't read my lips.

Afterwards, we lay on the rug, looking up at the cracked ceiling. She held her tattooed arms into the air and wiggled them, as if to show me how fine she was. "I had a premonition that I was going to die."

"Just now?"

"The other day. My Quick Pick numbers came up bad."

"You're playing the lottery?"

She nodded. It was something I had never known her to do in the past. She was a tattooed lottery player. My wife was only a memory of this woman.

"The numbers were bad. All fours."

"Fours?"

"Yeah. Seven in a row."

"I don't understand how the lottery works. Don't you pick the numbers?"

"The machine generates them."

"What machine?"

"The one at that BP near University Mall."

"Near the recycling bins?"

"Yeah."

"So that doesn't mean anything. That was some blip in the machine or something."

"All I'm saying is four has always meant bad things for me."

"What are you talking about?"

"When I was four, I got meningitis." It was why she was deaf.

"I spent the last two decades dealing with this craziness from Kaz, and look, what did you just tell me? That that stuff didn't even matter. If we could beat the Simon brothers without magic, you can buy a lottery ticket without dying."

I put my arm around her and my face back into her neck. Without her long hair tickling my face, it was more comfortable than it had ever been. No matter how familiar the furniture was, I'd never seen it from this angle before. All the pieces of my previous life were here, scarred, tattooed, and new. I fell asleep. When I awoke, the dust was still just barely lit with the last of the daylight, and one bird still sung in the pines outside. Anne was asleep on the floor beside me, and I let her stay there, pristine and naked and new.

I found Manny asleep in the driver's seat, his head leaned back against the headrest, the sun full on his face. I couldn't imagine ever being relaxed enough to sleep in direct sunlight on the side of a road while my friend had sex with his divorced wife a lawn away. I coughed. He opened one eye. "You single?"

I held up the papers.

"How'd it go?"

I nodded, nonchalant and slow.

"Single man ain't nothing but a big ole donkey dick waiting to lick the lamb!" Manny said. He started the Fiat and pulled into the road, then looked over at me and slammed on the brakes. "Look at me," he said. "*Look.*"

I looked at him.

He rubbed the sleep out of his eyes and said, "You sneaky motherfucker."

"What?"

"You just had divorce sex, didn't you?"

That night, while Manny slept on the floor in a sleeping bag that I had bought in high school, I walked back through the dark streets and stood by the fence at the edge of Anne's yard. Her windows were dark. I let the mosquitoes suck my blood while the benevolent insects stayed hidden, grinding the air into soft shredded bits with their frantic, pulsing song. Then the windows burst into a flash of light. Three blue rectangles hovered in my vision like lost ghosts across the lawn.

I had a note in my pocket written on unlined paper, folded eight times. Its thick, clumsy corners were already grubby. It said, WE CAN START OVER. It said, I KNOW THIS IS STUPID. It said, I DON'T CARE WHAT YOU DID. It said, I LOVE YOU! I couldn't remember the last time I'd written a note to anyone that said more than I'LL BE BACK IN TEN MINUTES. I approached the entrance of the fence and laid my finger atop the corner of one wooden picket. Just past the threshold the windows flashed again. I stopped, one foot past the gate. I envisioned Anne in her old nightgown, so thin you could see her breasts through its sheer fabric, lovely and smiling by herself, holding the camera's remote control at the end of the hallway. The neighbors stepped onto the stoop of their house, accompanied by a small black poodle on a leash. The dog bounced on its back legs and yapped in a torrent of alarm. I waved. Once we returned from Dubai, I would be living permanently within a half mile of Anne. We had our whole lives now, just blocks apart. I backed into the street. I didn't need to give her this note. I could tell her in person when it was right. The windows filled with the flash of another photo. *A note*, I thought. She would have laughed. I fingered one grubby corner in my pocket as I walked back home, through the thick, pulsing night, to my coach in a sleeping bag on my floor. I was hopeful. The future was a familiar landscape, just waiting to be revisited.

28

MRS. JACKSON WAS a large black woman who had looked forty years old for twenty-five years. She lived next door to Kaz in Midway and had been a cashier at the Kroger on Smith Level since I could remember. Throughout all of it she had smelled like coconut lotion.

"Slow," she said, lifting a banana to the red laser. "How come I didn't see you at the funeral?"

"For who?"

"These on sale?"

"Just regular."

"You kidding me?" The banana would not read.

"I've been out of town. Who?"

"Son." She held the banana against her large stomach. "You for real?"

"No. I mean, yeah."

"I hate to be the one to tell you. I sure do."

"What?"

"Miss Sue got up in a car wreck."

"Got up in one?"

"Sure did."

"Is she alright?"

"I said she ain't."

"What?"

"I said Sue passed away two Wednesdays back."

"Glover?"

"Don't you play with her boy?"

"Sort of."

"I'm sorry to be the one to tell you."

"I."

"He's a good son. He's been running that place all on his own."

"What place?"

"His mother China place."

"Sue-nami?"

"Yes sir. With his dad, but he ain't good for nothing." She put the banana into my bag without scanning it. "You go on and see him."

Two cats scurried away from Manny's Fiat as he flew down Rogerson Drive. He shot through a stop sign. He rumbled over a speed bump. Once, in the hospital during Anne's coma, a very tan nurse with multiple tattoos of roses and barbed wire had said, "Fuck cars. That's everything that comes in here is car wrecks. I'm serious. See that, that right there? So I'm like, fuck cars." But I didn't say anything to Manny. I felt like action was beyond consequence. When I drove, I drove like an old woman, yet I still almost killed my wife. Manny's recklessness seemed to run just as much risk. And then there was Sue. She had probably never gone over 55 in her life. And now she was dead.

I wanted to call Anne and tell her, but I was sure she already knew. Since our afternoon together on the floor of her cottage three days before, we had emailed twice, nothing more. It made me jealous that she hadn't told me about Sue. Part of me was confident Manny had heard and had kept the knowledge from me on purpose. We were leaving for Australia in days. He didn't want anything else on my mind.

We screeched into the lot at Sue-nami. Inside, the photos of me and Kaz still hung on the walls in the same spots on the same dusty nails.

"They need to take this shit down," Manny said. "They got like, what, your old chewing gum up here?"

A beautiful young Korean woman came to meet us at the entrance. If she recognized me from the photos on the wall she didn't say so. Manny clasped his hands together, bowed, and said, *"Hai."*

"Kaz working?" I said.

"Who?" she said.

"Kaz?"

"Mr. Glover?"

"Yeah."

She gave a small bow and, before gesturing to our table, receded into the kitchen. Manny and I sat at one of the tables centered with a large range, the ones from which Sue's chefs would flip shrimp tails up and into their hats, where they would dramatically knock salt shakers together as they juggled, and upon which they would light pools of cooking oil that would plume into the air in tongues of flame. The dining room was empty now, the other range-centered tables dark and cold.

Kaz stepped out of the kitchen. He wore a white apron over a white polyester shirt and pants. He had a towel over his shoulder and wore a drooping white pipe of a hat. I had seen him in whites thousands of times before, but this was different. With the yellowed forest wallpaper behind him, he looked like a Japanese butcher lost in the woods.

"Konichiwa, bitches," Manny said.

Kaz slowly approached.

"Check you out, brother," Manny said. "You're keeping it real."

"Hey," Kaz said. He took the hat off and let it dangle at his waist.

"We heard about your mom," I said.

"How you hanging?" Manny said.

"I'm alright," Kaz said.

"Loved that girl," Manny said. "Midway ain't never gonna see anyone like Sue Glover again. Ever."

Kaz nodded.

"How's your dad?" I said.

Kaz shook his head. "Had to get his other foot amputated."

"Jesus Christ."

"Ooof," Manny said.

"Diabetes."

"Where is he?"

"In the kitchen."

"Here?"

"Yeah, he's helping me out," Kaz said.

"What? He mixing up some oodles of noodles back there, sushi style?" Manny said.

Kaz laughed.

"We just came by to see how you were," I said.

"The fuck," Manny said. "We want some *menus*. We're going to eat all the rotten fish you got in this place."

I looked at him. Our plan was to pay our condolences and go. But that grin on his face said we weren't going anywhere.

When Kaz returned to the kitchen, Manny said, "That dude is keeping it *real*. He told me once when we were talking about Midway that doubles was his ticket out, but doubles ain't a way out of anywhere. What's fucked up is that this"—he held his hand out towards the empty dining room and the faded woods on the wall—"this is his ticket out."

An old black man in a white sweat suit rolled out of the kitchen in a wheelchair. He looked like a balled-up piece of leather. The prosthetic was gone. Both legs ended in stumps held in by sweatpants tied off at the ankles. He wheeled what was left of himself towards us. I was seized by nervousness. This was the man who had set me on my career path as a professional athlete. Nothing could have seemed less likely.

"Boys," he said, his voice a whisper through the residue of Kools.

"Mr. Glover," Manny said. "I'm so sorry."

"Sue loved you boys."

A lump rose in my throat. I breathed deeply.

"How'd you get that one, Mr. Glover?" Manny said. "How'd you fool her into coming back with you?"

Mr. Glover laughed. "She didn't have nowhere else to go."

"You did alright," Manny said.

Mr. Glover laughed again. He looked around. "She did alright. You boys eating?"

"Kaz's bringing out some menus," I said.

"Menus?" Mr. Glover said and waved a pink-palmed claw in the air. I was filled with relief. I'd never even seen a Sue-nami menu. I would have had no idea what to order. "It's good of you boys to come here. Where you been?"

"Casablanca."

"Woooo," Mr. Glover said, eyes opening wide. "That is the *life*."

In Casablanca it seemed like every wall was crumbling. In one building, paint fell off in chunks before my very eyes. The hotel I stayed in had broken windowpanes that let mosquitoes pour in all night. The civic infrastructure made getting to the courts a daily impossibility. If you did get through traffic, the cabs ripped you off. The organizers arranged for food that gave half the players immediate diarrhea. But there was no way I was going to tell all that to Mr. Glover.

"Of all the gin joints in all the world," Manny said, and Mr. Glover wheezed a breathy laugh.

"It is good to see you boys. Sure is."

He rolled past the woods back into the kitchen and left the late afternoon dining room to me and Manny. The young lady who had seated us turned on the range and set a large ceramic carafe of hot sake on it. Then soup. Then seaweed salad. That was the last of what

I could identify. Small plates with skewers of meat arrived. Dumplings filled with ground meat and spices. Spring rolls that looked like internal organs. Then the boat, filled with sushi in whites, oranges, blacks, reds, greens. Shrimp tails stood at attention. We ate it all. They sent a second boat. Manny's giant lips enveloped anything that came before them. I ate almost as much. At one point Manny mixed soy sauce with his sake and held it into the air. "It's all made of the same stuff," he said, then drank it.

Kaz emerged from the kitchen and said, "That *unagi* still as good?"

I didn't know what *unagi* was. But I nodded.

"Hell yeah," Manny said.

"Want more?"

"Yeah, but I can't fit it," Manny said. "Your mom was here, man, she'd walk this stuff out."

Kaz chuckled.

"Hey," Manny said. "You can do it. Walk on us." He lay on his stomach on the old dark carpet. "Slow, come here. Get down here."

I looked at Kaz.

"Slow!"

I lay on the floor beside my coach.

"Come on," Manny said. "Our food don't know what to do. Walk on us."

Kaz took off his shoes and tentatively stepped onto Manny, who unleashed a roar. Then he stepped on me. Each step felt dangerous. I had plans to go to Australia within the week. I couldn't throw out my back. But as Kaz made his way up and down our spines, both of us moaning and gasping, I started to relax. I opened my eyes and saw, through a hedge of carpet, Kaz's father in the light of the open kitchen door. He moved a cigarette in and out of his mouth.

At the door, Manny said, "We should do something sometime."

"Yeah," I said.

Kaz nodded vigorously.

"I'll call you," he said. "Yeah."

Manny and I drove through the crickets and the frogs and the wind without talking. We didn't need to. We had a trip to Australia to plan, hours in planes together and a few weeks in a hotel before it ended and we started over again back at the UNC tennis center. It hadn't been discussed, but I knew Kaz had heard we'd gotten the job.

That night, after Manny fell asleep, I walked into the cold January streets and watched my breath appear when I neared a streetlight, then fade from sight as I passed. I walked across Anne's lawn and knocked on her door. The neighbors stepped outside with their dog, and I waved. They stared at me like I was a stranger, because I was. I knocked again. No one answered.

29

I PULLED INTO the farthest corner of the parking lot behind Nice Price Books, near the corner of Main and Franklin. In summer the gravel space was buried deep in shade, perfect for keeping the Dart's black vinyl from searing flesh upon reentry. Now there was no sunlight to avoid and no Dart to guard. It was a gray February day, the kind that surprised new students who thought North Carolina had no winter at all. I pulled the Volvo into a space beside a small mound of ice-crusted leaves blown into the corner of a low retaining wall of railroad ties. Bare tree branches reached low around the roof. The car shuddered for several seconds after I turned it off, as if it still had places to go. I stepped out, and my breath thickened the air with steam. It had been a long time since I'd spent this much time in North Carolina during winter. It had snowed three days before. The streets were still white and chalky with the remnants of municipal salt. I tucked the back of my shirt into my jeans to keep out the cold air that kept creeping up my back. A wood fire burned somewhere, and I just stood there for a moment, breathing in that soft aroma on the back of the biting air.

They said that when the metal spring from the car seat finally dislodged itself from Anne's spine, it floated up and into her heart. Everyone said that, like her body was just some tub of water in which things floated up to a surface where her heart waited like a vacuum. She had died while Manny and I had been in Sydney.

We slept almost the whole trip back, afraid to be awake. I selfishly wondered whom she had told about the brakes. For a brief span of waking night over the Pacific I worried that her family would sue me for her death. I threw up during the layover in Hawaii. Her funeral was a small affair held at the museum. People treated me like we were still married. I think many of them had no idea that we weren't. Her father held my hand and told me I would always be a part of the family.

The night after her funeral, I drove to the BP by University Mall and bought a lottery ticket. I scratched off the pasty gold foil and found a jumble of unremarkable digits. For a brief moment I thought I'd hit the jackpot. It was the first lottery ticket I had ever bought. When I looked closer I saw that I had won $20.

Now there was an exhibition of Anne's photography inside the Carrboro ArtsCenter, over the railroad ties to my left. I had seen each of her projects emerge piece by piece, bit by incremental bit, so even if I didn't understand the aesthetics, I came to know the logic and the pace. This one had happened only blocks away, yet I had no idea what it was.

Familiar faces sucked on cigarettes along the sidewalk outside. A little girl waited for someone at the door, and for a second I thought that she too was smoking, but it was only the cold turning her breath into puffs of mist blossoming briefly from her lips. I waved to one of the smokers—Henry, who had gone to high school with Anne—who waved back without saying anything, his shoulders hunched under a heavy Army jacket. The entryway was crowded and hot. Inside I stripped off layers, piling them atop the disembodied jackets of others.

"Jim," I said, as another one of Anne's old classmates passed by. He was a tall, bearded PhD student who looked like he was straight out of central casting for tall, bearded PhD students. I had always liked him. He seemed the most down-to-earth of that whole crowd, some-one who probably watched football while reading Proust.

"Hey," he said. He looked stunned and uncomfortable. "How you doing?"

Somehow that's when I knew. I stepped into the exhibition space. Polaroids, evenly spaced, stretched around three walls like miniature windows. I could have guessed that much. But then I saw myself in one of those little frames. I stepped closer. In the photo my mouth was open, and I looked both scared and ecstatic. The white space said I JUST GOOGLED CLAIR HUXTABLE NAKED. Next to it was another. I looked almost exactly the same, in mid speech, animated and blurry. It said THE WRECK, IT WAS MY FAULT.

Hundreds of my secrets hung on the walls. The faces of Katie, Kaz, Manny, and Anne herself filled the other space. People stood in small packs, leaning in closely, reading and laughing. Saying, "Look at this." There was a group of people by one wall all holding one arm into the air. I walked back into the entranceway, collected my layers, and returned to the cold. In the car I held them to my chest, watching my breath crystallize on the inside of the windshield until I realized I'd forgotten to put them back on.

Just after midnight I returned. I parked in the same spot and crunched back across the frozen gravel. I cut around the back of the ArtsCenter, ducking under a metal sculpture of acute abstract angles. I kicked it by accident, and it rang hollow and low in the night. The back door was locked, but I had been here with Anne so many times in the past that I knew about the key hidden inside a piece of fake dog poop. The owner called it the doo-key. I found it behind a concrete planter filled with a miniature dead pine. Before I grasped it, I halted with the momentary fear that this doo-key was the real thing. But no dog could have fit himself behind the planter, so I let my fingers touch it, and it was hard and plastic, and it jingled. The loading dock was filled with dim red light from the EXIT. I flipped a switch, and one fluorescent tube flickered to life.

Almost all the photos looked the same. Just heads in midspeech, eyebrows raised, sometimes blurry. Closely cropped. I wasn't the only one who had allowed Anne to shoot. There were probably a dozen of Manny. I PUT RAT POISON IN MRS. REAGUE'S DIET COKE IN FOURTH GRADE. I LOVE JAMES TAYLOR. I DID IT IN THE BUTT WITH TISDALE GORDY. He looked thrilled in each photo, joyous with the attention.

Kaz's wall was more subdued. I CRIED WHEN I WATCHED THE LITTLE MERMAID. I PEED MY BED ONE NIGHT IN DUBAI.

Katie looked beautiful in her blurry photos, most taken inside her own apartment. Her secrets were insane. PRETTY OFTEN I THINK ABOUT HOW I'M THE COOLEST PERSON IN THE ROOM. I CROSS MY TOES FOR LUCK. I MASTURBATE LIKE ALMOST EVERY DAY.

Still, no matter what any of them said, I knew it all already. Even if I hadn't heard it before. Nothing was a surprise. Small square after small square, these lives had been lived together in a slow unpeeling of layers. I returned to my own photos. THE WRECK, IT WAS MY FAULT. I reached to the wall and took the photo into my hands.

A door on the loading dock slammed shut, and footsteps sounded light and slow across the floor. I took my cell phone out of my pocket and opened it, holding it in my other hand. The steps neared. I put the phone to my ear. I turned to the entryway and watched Kaz step into the gallery.

"One second," I said into the phone, then held it from me like some unseen person in some other place were inconvenienced by his intrusion. "Hey."

"What are you doing?" Kaz said, baffled. He had stopped only a few steps inside the gallery space.

"I'm on the phone. What are you doing?"

He breathed in deeply and sighed. "Um." He held his hand out towards the photos.

"How'd you get in?"

"Doo-key."

I nodded. I held the phone up, as if to say, *you know how it is*, then placed the dead machine back to my ear. "Listen," I said. "That sounds great. I'd love to play. Let me call you back, though. Alright. Bye."

I closed it and slid it into my pocket.

"Thanks for dinner the other night," I said.

"I'm doing the *unagi* better now."

"What *is unagi*?"

"You serious?" He said and walked farther into the gallery.

"I never ordered there."

"But it's not just served *there*. That's a standard thing."

I shrugged. Anywhere that it had ever been served, if I'd gone there, it had been with Kaz. He had always ordered.

"Eel," he said, an afterthought as he read one of Katie's secrets. "I meant to say congrats."

"On what?"

"The job."

"It's not all that."

He turned to the photos of himself on the wall.

"You know those were going to be here?" I said.

"She told me."

"You see her much?" I said. I didn't know if I wanted to know.

"Some," Kaz said. "You?"

"Some," I said, suddenly positive I'd seen less of her than Kaz. "She told me about charades."

Kaz turned.

I said, "In New York last year."

He waited for a second, as if trying to determine if it was yet safe to tell the truth. "Yeah." He nodded. "We just went home."

"So it was just us."

"What was?"

"That won."

His eyes lit up his thin, dark face, and for a moment I wished I was half Japanese and half black. He looked like the coolest guy in Chapel Hill. "Yeah," he said. "We won."

I laughed. One short puff.

Then he said, "You taking one?"

I looked at the photo in my hands. I held it out to him. He took it gingerly, looked down, nodded, and handed it back.

"You knew?" I said.

He nodded. "She told me."

I glanced at a few more of myself. I THROW AWAY THE NEWSPAPER SOMETIMES, NOT IN THE RECYCLING. I TEXT WITH MY EX-GIRLFRIEND. I couldn't imagine anything possibly making a difference anymore. I hung the photo back on the wall.

Kaz said, "See these?"

He stood in front of the photos of Anne. I expected them all to be taken by me. The dress in the clothes bin, the fliers for Winnie under the carpet. But those photos were missing. These were self-portraits taken in an unfamiliar room. Different days, I could tell, and different light, but in each Anne sat beside a window, the light falling half-way onto her. In her lap she held the camera remote, its cord reaching taut towards the frame like she might connect the viewer to the photo by reeling us in. Her mouth was moving and in every single one she looked confident and relaxed. The first one said, COUNT TO NINE. Then there were nine photos, a digit at the bottom of each. The next said, IMAGINE THROWING SOMETHING INTO THE AIR. The next said, WATCH IT RISE. KEEP THAT ARM RAISED. The next said, I'M GOING TO

TELL YOU A SECRET. I turned to look at Kaz. His arm was high above his head. So was mine. We had both thrown an invisible tennis ball into that vast silent room. And then each photo after that had the same caption written on it, like she was testing the secret for validity, day by day by day.

They said I LOVE YOU. I LOVE YOU. I LOVE YOU. I LOVE YOU.

About the Author

NIC BROWN'S FIRST book, *Floodmarkers*, was published in 2009 and selected as an Editor's Choice by *The New York Times Book Review*. His short stories have appeared in the *Harvard Review*, *Glimmer Train*, and *Epoch*, among many other publications. A graduate of Columbia University and the Iowa Writers' Workshop, he teaches at the University of Northern Colorado.